Alexander stood his ground as the boys slowed and stopped . . .

"You don't expect us to believe you're going to take the blame for smashing that bookcase without trying to get back at us, do you?" Kim's eyes narrowed in a dark scowl.

"Believe what you want," Alexander countered.

"Don't play dumb with us, Alexander," Bernard snapped. "No self-respecting Klingon would let us off the hook."

"That's right. Don't you Klingons have this thing about defending your *ho-nor.*"

Bernard put a ridiculing emphasis on the word that made Alexander bristle. Still, he held his temper even as the impatient fury sparked. "You don't know anything about honor, Bernard."

"Maybe you don't, either." Jeremy took a daring step forward. "Maybe you didn't snitch because you knew *we'd* do something about it."

Gritting his teeth, Alexander fought the terrible, burning desire to rip the smug, challenging sneer off Jeremy's face.

STAR TREK
DEEP SPACE NINE®
DAY OF HONOR
HONOR BOUND

DIANA G. GALLAGHER

Interior illustrations by
Gordon Purcell

A MINSTREL® BOOK

Published by POCKET BOOKS
New York   London   Toronto   Sydney   Tokyo   Singapore

A MINSTREL PAPERBACK *Original*

A Minstrel Book published by
POCKET BOOKS, a division of Simon & Schuster Inc.
1230 Avenue of the Americas, New York, NY 10020

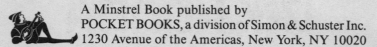

STAR TREK is a Registered Trademark of Paramount Pictures.

A VIACOM COMPANY

This book is published by Pocket Books, a division of Simon & Schuster Inc., under exclusive license from Paramount Pictures.

ISBN: 0-671-01452-8

First Minstrel Books printing October 1997

10 9 8 7 6 5 4 3 2 1

A MINSTREL BOOK and colophon are registered trademarks of Simon & Schuster Inc.

Cover art by Michael Herring

Printed in the U.S.A.

*With respect and affection
for Ray Sehgal,
a brilliant young scientist
and my youngest Trek advisor*

With special thanks to
L. A. Graf
for providing invaluable information
from "Armageddon Sky"
in the interest of consistency
concerning the Day of Honor rites and rules

STARFLEET TIMELINE

2264

The launch of Captain James T. Kirk's five-year mission, _U.S.S. Enterprise,_ NCC-1701.

2292

Alliance between the Klingon Empire and the Romulan Star Empire collapses.

2293

Colonel Worf, grandfather of Worf Rozhenko, defends Captain Kirk and Doctor McCoy at their trial for the murder of Klingon chancellor Gorkon.

Khitomer Peace Conference, Klingon Empire/Federation (_Star Trek VI_).

2323

Jean-Luc Picard enters Starfleet Academy's standard four-year program.

2328

The Cardassian Empire annexes the Bajoran homeworld.

2346

Romulan massacre of Klingon outpost on Khitomer.

2351

In orbit around Bajor, the Cardassians construct a space station that they will later abandon.

2363

Captain Jean-Luc Picard assumes command of _U.S.S. Enterprise,_ NCC-1701-D.

2367

Wesley Crusher enters Starfleet Academy.

An uneasy truce is signed between the Cardassians and the Federation.

Borg attack at Wolf 359; First Officer Lieutenant Commander Benjamin Sisko and his son, Jake, are among the survivors.

U.S.S. Enterprise-D defeats the Borg vessel in orbit around Earth.

2369

Commander Benjamin Sisko assumes command of Deep Space Nine in orbit over Bajor.

2371

U.S.S. Enterprise, NCC-1701-D, destroyed on Veridian III.

Former Enterprise captain James T. Kirk emerges from a temporal nexus, but dies helping Picard save the Veridian system.

U.S.S. Voyager, under the command of Captain Kathryn Janeway, is accidentally transported to the Delta Quadrant. The crew begins a 70-year journey back to Federation space.

2372

The Klingon Empire's attempted invasion of Cardassia Prime results in the dissolution of the Khitomer peace treaty between the Federation and the Klingon Empire.

Source: Star Trek® Chronology / Michael Okuda and Denise Okuda

HONOR BOUND

CHAPTER 1

Alexander Rozhenko was one-quarter human, three-quarters Klingon and totally furious!

Sitting between his human grandparents in the shuttle terminal at Earth Station Bobruisk, Alexander stubbornly refused to look them in the eye. He didn't want to relax or listen to reason. He didn't want to see the troubled patience in Sergey Rozhenko's eyes or the disappointment his grandmother hid behind a stoical smile. But he especially didn't want to see his father, Worf.

"I don't understand this hostility toward your father, Alexander," Sergey said gently.

"Nor do I." Helena sighed with deep sorrow. "Worf is taking special leave from his duties on *Deep Space Nine* just to come see you. So you can celebrate the Klingon Day of Honor together. You were so upset when he canceled his vacation plans to visit Earth, we thought you'd be happy."

Alexander's upper lip curled in a snarl, a low, guttural

expression of displeasure that was distinctly and uncomfortably Klingon. It was the kind of Klingon trait he usually struggled to suppress. Now, he didn't bother to try. He resented his grandparents' patronizing attitude toward him.

"He is taking *emergency* leave, and it's not because he wants to celebrate his sacred Klingon holiday with me!" Eyes flashing, Alexander snapped his gaze from his grandfather to his grandmother, then focused straight ahead. "My father is taking time away from his duty because *you* asked him to come."

Catching the worried glance that passed between the elderly couple, Alexander choked back the hurtful words he was about to add. It wasn't fair to take his anger out on his grandparents. That made about as much sense as blaming the Romulans who had attacked the Khitomer Outpost in 2346. If they had killed his father instead of leaving him alive at the age of six, Sergey and Helena Rozhenko wouldn't have adopted the orphaned Klingon and they wouldn't be saddled with a problem they couldn't handle now— him—their mostly Klingon grandson. Desperate, the Rozhenkos had turned to the one person in the Federation who might be able to help: Lieutenant Commander Worf, Strategic Operations Officer on *Deep Space Nine* and the only Klingon in Starfleet.

Sergey glanced at the time. "Worf's shuttle should be landing in a few minutes."

Alexander stiffened when the old man gripped his shoulder.

"At least try to be civil, Alexander." Removing his hand, Sergey spoke sternly. "Regardless of your mis-

2

guided feelings right now, Worf is your father and you *will* treat him with respect."

Bristling, Alexander clenched his fists and concentrated on the steady movement of air in and out of his lungs. His grandfather rarely used that commanding tone of voice with him. In the past, Alexander would have felt ashamed and sorry for whatever he had done to deserve it. This time, it took every ounce of his willpower not to attack the old man.

In. Out. In. Out.

Alexander breathed, calming the explosive urge, but not the emotional torment he felt. His mother, K'Ehleyr, had been half-human and the Federation ambassador to the K'mpec government in the Klingon Empire before she was murdered by Duras. Like her, Alexander had embraced human behavior and customs with all his heart and soul. Now his cherished human value system and code-of-conduct was being threatened by a passion for violence that surged through his veins like a virus.

Alexander didn't know why, but he had suddenly become prone to enraged fits of temper that were getting harder to control. He was terrified that one day he wouldn't be able to stop himself and someone would get hurt. What he feared most was that the victim of his fury would be his beloved grandfather or grandmother.

And for that reason alone, Alexander was glad his father had agreed to visit Earth. He would rather die than bring harm to the kindly couple that had given him a loving home as they had his father before him. His disruptive behavior had already caused his grandparents more heartache and worry than he cared to admit. The

Rozhenkos did not have much to say about Worf's adolescent years, either, which made him suspect that his own faults were a lot worse than his father's had been.

Worf must have been a model child compared to him.

And that thought caused another spasm of intense anger to rise within him.

"It's here." Helena stood up. Anxious and excited, she gazed at the door where the disembarking passengers from the shuttlecraft *von Braun* would soon enter.

Nudging his sullen grandson to his feet, Sergey smiled tightly. "There is one thing you must never forget, Alexander. Worf loves you very much and nothing you do or say can change that."

Alexander nodded curtly, still avoiding his grandfather's gaze. He was certain of his father's feelings, too, but with a twist that Sergey didn't understand. Worf was Klingon and Klingons valued honor above all. His father had made *that* perfectly clear when he had gone back to the *Enterprise* to live after spending a year on Earth following his mother's death.

Alexander thought back to the traumatic and uncertain beginnings of his relationship with Worf. Even then, he had become too much of a discipline problem for the aging Rozhenkos to handle. Deanna Troi, the counselor aboard the starship, had recognized that his disgraceful lies and disruptive behavior were expressions of his feelings of loss and insecurity. Worf had understood and had decided not to send him to a Klingon school as he had planned. Being forgiven and accepted by his father had given him the stability he needed to resolve his emotional problems and explore his mixed heritage.

But I'm not a scared little kid anymore, Alexander thought dismally, and I don't have an acceptable excuse this time. Dragged away from his post on *Deep Space Nine* to deal with his unruly son, Worf would feel angry, betrayed and dishonored. Love didn't matter.

Bracing himself, Alexander watched the door as a stream of human and alien travelers walked through. Most of them were civilians and families returning from business trips or vacations on other worlds. An occasional flash of Starfleet red, blue or yellow caused the breath to catch in his throat before the silver sheen of the Klingon sash his father wore caught his eye.

Alexander couldn't help but feel a sense of awe as the imposing Klingon moved into view. Tall and muscular with an expression that always seemed grim, Worf paused in the doorway to scan the crowded waiting area. The human family ahead of him fumbled with bundles of souvenirs and carry-on baggage. He did not seem to notice the nervous glances the man and woman cast over their shoulders at him as they frantically tried to get out of his way. In fact, Alexander realized, everyone in the waiting area was giving him a wide berth and watching him suspiciously.

Which was no surpise to Alexander.

Hostilities had broken out between the Federation and the Klingon Empire after decades of peace. The tenuous alliance had dissolved when Gowron led a Klingon attack against the Cardassian Empire, believing it had been infiltrated by the Dominion. Starfleet had defended the Cardassians, an insult and breach of faith the Klingon Empire could not ignore even though Gowron had started the conflict because he was afraid and misinformed.

6

Worf, a Starfleet officer, had fought against the Klingons, but the uniform he wore with such fierce pride, evidence of his loyalty to the Federation, might as well have been invisible now. A mere piece of black and red cloth could not negate Worf's genetic heritage.

Or mine, Alexander thought dismally.

The boy wondered if his father was aware of the hostile shunning he would experience on Earth because he was a Klingon. Since the beginning of the break between the Empire and the Federation, Alexander's life at school and in the neighborhood had become a nightmare. His uncontrollable temper had flared up about the same time. He assumed the tantrums were provoked by the cruel and unjust actions and attitudes of his peers.

"Worf!" Helena waved and called to her adopted son. "Over here!"

Alexander tensed as his father greeted them with a slight nod. There was no warmth in the hard eyes that met his son's equally hard stare. As the boy expected, the reunion was not going to be pleasant. He had not even realized he was harboring a faint hope that Worf would be glad to see him. The unspoken rejection made his blood burn with a feverish fury.

"My boy!" Grinning, Sergey rushed forward, accidently brushing against the human man scurrying out of Worf's path. "Excuse me. I'm—"

"Watch where you're going!" The man's son, a large, husky boy about Alexander's age, shoved Sergey aside. "Klingon lover!"

Helena gasped and steadied Sergey as he stumbled into her.

"Howard!" The boy's father snapped, then paled.

The boy glared at the Rozhenkos.

Worf's eyes flashed and his lip quivered in a silent snarl. Every muscle in his powerful body tightened, poised to strike the boy who had pushed Sergey, but he did not attack.

In the fraction of a second Worf paused to calm himself, and everyone else in the area became frozen in shocked fear, Alexander reacted with pure Klingon rage.

Roaring, Alexander sprang toward Howard with his clawed hands aimed at the fragile human throat. The fury coursing through his young body blinded him to everything except the need to destroy the arrogant, offensive boy. Howard had insulted and shoved one of the few people in the galaxy Alexander loved.

"Alexander! No!"

Alexander barely heard his grandmother's scream as he tackled the stunned boy, knocking him to the ground. A strong hand gripped his arm, pulling him off the shrieking human before his fingers closed around tender flesh.

"That is enough!" Worf barked.

"Get him away!" Howard squealed as he scooted backward, then scrambled to his feet. "Get him away!"

Infused with strength as the savagery locked in his Klingon genes erupted, Alexander ripped free of the hand that held him.

Screeching with terror, Howard ran.

"Alexander!"

As Alexander gave chase, Worf's demanding voice was lost in the thunder of his own blood pounding in his ears. He was only vaguely aware of the alien-dotted, human sea parting before him or the shouts of those pursuing him. He was totally focused on the panicked boy fleeing through the terminal.

Leaping luggage and darting between supporting pillars and rows of seats, Alexander quickly closed the distance between himself and his prey. The stench of human fear flooded his nostrils, feeding the hunter frenzy that drove him. A terminal security guard jumped into the aisle ahead. Dodging to the right, Alexander shoved the man and ran past.

Howard looked back as the guard thudded against the wall. Eyes widening in fear, he stumbled over his own feet and sprawled on the tiled floor.

The cry of victory rising in Alexander's throat as he lunged toward the boy was abruptly silenced. A hand with a grip like iron clamped around his arm, stopping him dead in his tracks. He fought against the hold, but this time he could not break free.

"Alexander."

The calm, commanding sound of his father's voice broke through the fury. Pulse racing, Alexander blinked and tried to still his rapid breathing. Through a slowly clearing fog he saw Howard's parents help him up and draw him into the comfort of their arms. Then his grandmother's arms were around him, holding him close as she murmured soothing sounds into his ear. He buried his face against her chest and began to shake.

If he had caught Howard, he might have killed him.

A strong, but gentle hand gripped his shoulder. Alexander looked up, expecting his father to be furious, but there was no anger in the warm brown eyes that gazed down on him. Worf's face softened with relief and worry and a tight-lipped smile of reassurance.

Stunned, Alexander did not immediately realize that the deep, unfamiliar voice he heard next was addressing him.

"You're under arrest."

CHAPTER 2

It'll be all right, Alexander," Helena whispered. "You'll see."

Alexander nodded and managed a wan smile to please his grandmother, but he was sure nothing would ever be all right again. He sat on one side of the Terminal Security Office with the Rozhenkos. Howard Chupek and his mother sat on the other side. Mr. Chupek and Worf stood stiffly before the chief of security's desk.

Like two Starfleet Academy cadets on report, Alexander thought glumly. Any chance there had been of closing the emotional gap between himself and his father was gone now. Worf would never forgive him for this embarrassment. Just as the sins of the father brought dishonor to the child in Klingon society, the sins of the child dishonored the father.

"I see no reason why this unfortunate situation can not be settled rationally." Worf's deep base voice resounded through the small room even though he spoke with calm reserve.

"Rationally?" Mr. Chupek blustered. "That Klingon spitfire of yours would have ripped Howard apart if you hadn't stopped him, Mr. Worf!"

Howard glanced at Alexander with a triumphant smirk. The smug smile disappeared when Alexander countered with a menacing stare.

"My *son* was defending his grandfather," Worf argued quietly. "I do not condone Alexander's methods, Mr. Chupek. However, we would not be here now if your son had not insulted and pushed my father to begin with."

Security Chief Clausen flicked an anxious gaze between the two fathers. He seemed concerned that they might pick up the fight where the boys had left off.

"Your father?" The man frowned uncertainly.

"That is correct." Shifting his attention back to Chief Clausen, Worf used Mr. Chupek's confused silence to press the advantage. "My son is going through a phase that is difficult for a young Klingon under ordinary circumstances."

What does he mean by "phase"? Alexander shifted uncomfortably, losing all interest in Howard. He didn't think of himself as a Klingon. The idea that he might not be able to stop acting like one was very disturbing.

"And your point, Lieutenant Commander Worf?" Chief Clausen prodded cautiously.

"Present hostilities between the Federation and the Empire are compounding the . . ." Worf hesitated, groping for an acceptable word. ". . . problem. Howard Chupek's insulting actions are a perfect example of why this is so."

"My son may have exercised poor judgment," Mr. Chupek said hotly, "but an insult hardly justifies your son's violent behavior!"

12

Alexander tensed and clenched his teeth. His grandmother's hand closed over his wrist, an alarming reminder that the rage could escape if he let down his guard for even an instant.

"The boy was provoked." A glint of warning flared in Worf's eyes, but he remained in total control.

"Mr. Chupek," Chief Clausen said sternly. "I would prefer to resolve this incident without causing irreparable harm to either boy. I'd appreciate it if you'd allow Mr. Worf to finish without further interruption."

Mr. Chupek nodded, but his cheeks flamed red.

"Thank you, Chief Clausen," Worf said. "I have come to Earth for the sole purpose of helping Alexander adjust to certain changes in his life. If you will release him into my custody, I give you my word as a Starfleet officer that he will cause no further trouble."

"Not if I have anything to say about it!" Mr. Chupek bellowed. Placing his hands on the desk, he glared at the security chief. "I'm pressing charges against that alien delinquent for assault with intent to do bodily harm! You can't just release him on this—this Klingon's word!"

Alexander inhaled sharply, expecting his father to lash out at the human who dared question his given word. It wasn't because he was a Starfleet officer, either. It was a matter of Klingon honor.

A Klingon's word is his bond. Without it he is nothing.

Worf would rather die than break an oath. Alexander didn't understand why his father clung so fervently to this as well as other rigid Klingon traditions, but he did. In Klingon society, Mr. Chupek's reckless accusation— that Worf would not do as he promised—would have triggered an attack that might have cost the imprudent man his life. But the only evidence of his father's intense indignation was a squaring of the shoulders and a narrowed, penetrating stare.

Chief Clausen was not easily intimidated, either.

"You are quite wrong in that regard, Mr. Chupek." Rising, the security man's scowl faded as he turned to Worf. "Since no one was injured, no property was damaged and both boys were instrumental in causing the incident, I'll let Alexander go with a warning this time. Take your son home, Mr. Worf."

Mr. Chupek sputtered, too angry to speak.

Sergey nodded in approval.

Helena squeezed Alexander's arm and smiled. "See? I told you it would work out."

Alexander just stared in disbelief. The security chief's leniency surprised him almost as much as his father's defense and request on his behalf. He had been positive that Worf would insist he take responsibility for his outrageous conduct and pay whatever penalty the law required.

Then again, Alexander thought, as Worf executed a stiff bow and turned away from Chief Clausen to face him. *Maybe he preferred to make me pay in some horrible Klingon ritual that was far worse than anything Federation law would demand.* He had seen that frustrated frown on his father's face too often when they had lived together on the *Enterprise.*

Worf gestured toward the door and waited for the Rozhenkos and Alexander to go first.

Getting to his feet, Alexander gladly turned his back on his father to leave. Worf's dark, unblinking eyes were as cold as the ridged Klingon face was impassive. The troubles he had blindly plunged into when he had rushed to his grandfather's defense were far from over. They were just beginning.

Flanked by his grandparents and with his father watching every move from behind, Alexander felt like a condemned prisoner being marched through the terminal. No one spoke, which only added to his anxiety. By the time they had picked up his father's duffel bag and arrived at the local shuttle stand, his nerves were dangerously on edge. Slipping into the front seat of the vehicle, he sat in brooding silence while his father programmed the Rozhenkos' residential coordinates into the automated navigation system.

Helena leaned forward as the shuttle lifted off the ground. "I'm making your favorite dinner tonight, Worf."

Worf glanced back. *"Rokeg* blood pie?"

"What else?" Sergey shuddered with disgust. "I still haven't acquired a taste for it. Never will, either."

"I'm making a pot roast, too, Sergey," Helena said, patting her husband's knee. "You can tell your stomach to relax."

Laughing, Worf settled back to watch the green hills and valleys of the Russian landscape skim by below.

The family small talk and ensuing quiet strained Alexander's nerves even further. His grandparents were chattering about Klingon glop for dinner as though his father had just dropped by for a casual visit instead of coming halfway across the galaxy to deal with him. His life was falling apart and everyone was acting like nothing was wrong.

As the shuttle began its descent over Mirnee Doleena, Alexander squirmed in his seat. Staring down at the small town where he lived and went to school stoked the fires. Mirnee Doleena translated as Peaceful Valley and the community had been exactly that when he had come to live with his grandparents on Earth again. But the town was not a welcoming, tranquil haven anymore. Between the Federation's renewed conflict with the Klingon Empire and his own uncontrollable temper, the local population had reason to despise him. Consequently, he had to cope with the vicious prejudice of strangers he met on the street as well as intolerant classmates who had once been his friends.

Alexander didn't blame them, but it was impossible to ignore the unfair and painful torment. He didn't have anything to do with the troubles between the Federation and the Empire and he had *chosen* to embrace his humanity in spite of his predominantly Klingon heritage. The rages were as much his enemy as anyone's.

Except for him, there was nowhere to run to escape them.

Like now.

He could feel his temper racing toward critical mass. He had to get away from his father and grandparents long enough to calm down—or until the rage ran its course.

Struggling to contain the anger, Alexander slammed his hand against the door latch when the shuttle touched down on the drive leading up to the Rozhenkos' modest house. As the door *whooshed* open, he sprang out and started to run toward the tall trees bordering the front lawn.

"Alexander!"

Worf yelled as Alexander leaped over his grandmother's carefully tended bed of brilliantly colored rosebushes. He reacted instinctively to his father's sharp command and whirled as he landed.

"Alexander, wait." Rushing around the front of the shuttle, Worf paused, then slowly advanced.

"It's all right, Alexander," Sergey pleaded as he stepped down from the rear compartment. "We're not angry with you."

But Alexander *was* angry and the rage deafened him to the concerned words. Feeling cornered and pushed to the limit, he gave in to the overwhelming fury.

A fury that was getting more violent and powerful with each outburst.

A fury that had to have an outlet.

Alexander attacked the only thing within reach. Screeching, he pulled Helena's prized hybrid rosebush out of the ground by the roots and tore it apart. Delicate yellow petals and green leaves rained on the grass around him. Sharp thorns dug into his skin, drawing blood. He did not even notice the pain until he tightened his grip on the main stem. A large thorn drove into his palm, piercing the enraged daze as effectively as it had pierced his tender flesh. His mind cleared in an agonizing instant.

Alexander stared at the demolished remains of the rosebush in shock. Limp roots dangled from the trunk he still held in his hand. Looking up, he saw his grandparents and his father staring back.

Worf's jaw flexed.

Sergey's gentle eyes filled with stunned pain.

Helena's hand covered her mouth and her face was ghostly pale. The glorious Butter Beauty Rose she had cultivated, pruned and raised with such pride and loving care was dead.

And he had killed it.

Dropping the thorned trunk, Alexander ran. This time, his father's booming voice could not call him back.

CHAPTER 3

Although the Rozhenkos' house was within walking distance of the small town, it was nestled on the edge of an expansive forest. Alexander sped across the lawn and darted into the cover of the thick woods. His worst fear had been realized. Destroying his grandmother's favorite rosebush was almost as bad as attacking Helena herself.

Avoiding the deer trails he and his grandfather used on their morning and evening strolls, Alexander drove deeper into the forest. The sound of Worf and Sergey's calling voices became muffled by the dense foliage, then faded completely into the quiet of the wilderness. Ashamed and confused, he kept running. Not because he was afraid of being yelled at or punished. He simply couldn't face the hurt and disappointment in his grandmother's eyes or his father's Klingon judgment.

Dry leaves crackled under Alexander's pounding feet. Brambles and broken branches scratched his skin and ripped his jumpsuit as he crashed through overgrown tangles of brush. Jumping from one moss-covered rock to another to cross a wide stream, he slipped and fell. Snarling with frustration as he scrambled to his feet, he plunged through the rushing water and clawed his way up the far bank. Mud and leaves clung to his wet hands, clothes and hair, but he ignored the discomfort. The thunder of water cascading over rocks in the woods upstream called to the savage essence of his Klingon blood, and he ran toward it.

Heart thudding against his ribs and breathless, Alexander finally stopped when his sleeve snagged on a young tree. Freeing himself, he sank to his knees a short distance from the high, roaring waterfall and focused on the spindly tree that was struggling to survive in the dim light. The canopy of leaves crowning its towering parent blocked the sun. His rage and energy spent, Alexander was suddenly consumed by a sorrowful empathy with the frail sapling.

Sighing with despair, Alexander sat and dropped his head into his folded arms. When he sensed his father moving through the forest and heard him call, he did not look up or try to flee.

"Alexander." Worf strode through the trees to stand before him. "We must talk."

"Just go away and leave me alone."

Worf stood his ground. "You are not to blame for what happened today. I am."

Alexander looked up sharply. "No, you're not! I'm the one who chased Howard Chupek through the terminal and tore up Grandma's rosebush!"

Nodding, Worf eased his bulk down onto a nearby log. "Do you know why?"

"Yeah! Because I'm a Klingon and Klingons are

always mad and want to fight all the time!" Tears stung Alexander's eyes.

"That is not true," Worf said. "A race that was always mad and fought *all* the time wouldn't survive."

"What's happening to me isn't funny!" In the past, his father's attempt at humor would have both surprised and amused Alexander. Now, it was a dangerous annoyance that poked and prodded the anger.

"I was not trying to be funny," Worf said calmly. "Even the Klingon Empire needs farmers and craftsmen. If everyone fought constantly, nothing would get done. We would still be prowling the forests with wooden spears."

"So Klingon farmers don't get mad?" Alexander asked sarcastically.

"I did not say that." Worf paused to eye Alexander with thoughtful concern. "We are a highly aggressive race. It is in our blood, the core of what we are—of who you are. But it is not the end of the world. Every problem has a solution and this one is no different."

"Oh, yeah! How would you know?" Jumping to his feet, Alexander glared at his father. Worf was talking to him with the calm understanding he had always wanted when they were together on the *Enterprise*. Why was he suddenly so furious with him? Bewildered and frustrated, Alexander started to pace.

"I know because I am a Klingon, too."

Alexander kept walking, too intent on fighting his mounting agitation to respond.

"Your body is going through some intense physical changes because you are growing up," Worf explained. "And those changes are causing these violent outbursts."

"So *that's* what you meant by 'phase' in Chief Clausen's office."

"Yes." Worf's face clouded slightly, as though he had momentarily drifted off to another place. "Every young Klingon experiences difficulty controlling the impulses that make them great warriors."

"So I'm *stuck* with being like this?" This was something he had suspected since the violent tantrums had begun a few weeks ago, but having his father confirm the awful truth out loud was a shock anyway. There was one thing he had always been sure of, something he had told his father when they had first started getting to know each other. He didn't *want* to be a warrior!

The emotional impact unlocked still more of Alexander's innate Klingon traits. His blood burned hotter, enhancing his senses. Every leaf and twig came into sharp focus and every nuance of sound rang crystal clear in his ears. The tang of decaying leaves and pungent fungi teased his nose, making him keenly aware of every subtle scent rising on the still air.

Worf started slightly. "You are *stuck* with your Klingon genes—"

His father's voice blended with the forest sounds, unheard as Alexander's attention was drawn to an enticing aroma.

Warm muscle and fur.

Prey.

A rabbit crouched in the thicket to the left, still except for the twitching nose and the quiet heaving of its life's breath.

"—but that does not mean you can not conquer the impulses they generate."

The scent of fear was irresistible. With every muscle

23

tensed and primed, Alexander savored the anticipation coursing through his hunter veins for a moment before he sprang. With a quickness and agility he did not know he had, he snatched the cowering rabbit from the brush. His own chest heaving with exhilaration, he clutched the fear-frozen animal by the throat and whirled to face his father.

"Your skills are excellent, Alexander. If we were on a ritual hunt, I would be very proud of your prowess." Rising slowly, Worf stepped forward. "Are you hungry?"

The blunt question disrupted Alexander's feeling of triumph but did not dampen the instinct to hunt and kill. His pulse raced and his hand tightened around the prey's fragile neck. It would be so easy to squeeze the life out of the dangling body, but his mind rebelled against causing a senseless death.

"No—" Alexander's voice was a harsh rasp. "I'm not hungry."

"Then why are you holding that rabbit in a death grip?"

Because I want to kill it! Alexander trembled as reason battled the genetic instincts within him. *But I don't want to kill it!*

"We are not on a ritual hunt designed to test your skills," Worf continued evenly. "There is no feast being planned to make use of the kill and you are not hungry."

Alexander focused on his father's voice.

"There is no honor in taking a life without purpose. Killing to vent anger or frustration is meaningless. Do you understand?"

Desperate, Alexander nodded, but he did not release the rabbit. His hand wanted to choke the terrified

animal. His mind wanted to see it go free. He stood frozen with indecision, trapped between his primitive impulses and his civilized values with the hapless rabbit's life hanging in the balance.

"Do you want to let the rabbit go?"

Again Alexander just nodded. He was afraid to move because his Klingon blood might overwhelm his desire. The rabbit could die in his hand in an instant and death could not be undone. There would be no second chances.

"Concentrate on your hand, Alexander. It is merely an extension of you. A tool that does your bidding, nothing more." Speaking in a soothing monotone, Worf held Alexander's frightened gaze. "You command the tool, Alexander. Open your hand."

Shaking with the effort, Alexander loosened his grip. The rabbit stirred slightly. The movement tempted the hunter and the hand flexed to close again. Beads of sweat broke out on his ridged forehead as he concentrated, forcing himself to squat down, to keep his killing hold in check.

"Remove your hand, Alexander. You control it and it will do as you command."

Lowering the captive rabbit to the ground, Alexander stared at his father while he focused his will on his hand. His fingers snapped open. Stunned and limp with fear, the animal did not immediately dash for safety. It just lay there in his open hand, taunting the hunter and testing his rational will.

And then it was gone.

Gasping, Alexander collapsed as the rabbit darted into the brush and fled.

Worf dropped to one knee on the ground beside him.

"There is a solution and you have just taken the first step. By letting the rabbit go, you have proven that *you* are the master of your actions and your destiny. Your Klingon blood cannot control you."

Pulling himself up into a sitting position, Alexander sighed wearily. "It almost did. You don't know how hard it was not to strangle that rabbit."

"Yes, I do," Worf said sympathetically. "It will not be an easy fight, but it *is* a fight you can win."

I sure hope so, Alexander thought. The rabbit's escape was too narrow for comfort and a sickening sensation churned in his stomach. The Klingon warrior impulses were more powerful than he had imagined and they were getting steadily stronger.

What if he couldn't learn to control it without fail?

There had been too many times in the past few weeks he had wanted to silence Jeremy Sullivan's taunting insults by strangling him.

CHAPTER 4

The next morning at breakfast, Alexander was all too aware that his grandparents were trying extra hard not to do anything to upset him.

And that upset him.

If he was a human kid and not mostly Klingon, they wouldn't be afraid that he might take offense at some innocent remark or minor incident and go berserk.

"Be careful, Alexander," Helena said as she set a plate of freshly baked biscuits on the table. "I just took them out of the oven and they're still hot."

Nodding, Alexander stared at the biscuits his grandmother still made the old-fashioned way. They had a replicator, but she preferred to measure and mix all the ingredients herself. Famished, he couldn't wait for the steaming biscuits to cool. He picked one up, inhaled with a hiss and dropped it on his plate.

Sergey tensed with a fork full of fried potatoes poised before his open mouth, staring at him as though he might fly into a rage and demolish the kitchen.

Helena smiled tightly. "Do you want some ice for the burn?"

Alexander shook his head and gritted his teeth to quell an angry outburst. He was not angry because he had been stupid enough to burn himself. Or at the Rozhenkos because they expected him to react violently. He was furious with the Klingon genes that triggered the tantrums and gave his grandparents good reason to worry.

And because there was nothing he could do about it.

"You didn't make any plans for today, did you?" Slipping the potatoes into his mouth, Sergey chewed and glanced at Alexander.

"Of course he didn't." Gently cuffing Sergey's shoulder, Helena sat down. "He knew his father was coming."

Alexander sighed. Not long ago deciding between spending the time with Worf or with his friends would have been a problem. However, it had been ages since he had gone to see the latest holoflick or participated in a casual game of soccer or just sat around the Galactic Cafe in town stuffing himself. Hanging out alone wasn't fun and none of his old friends were talking to him.

"No, I don't have any plans." Picking up the dropped biscuit, Alexander buttered it. "Why?"

"Well—" Sergey swallowed. "Worf thought you might like to join him for his *Mok'bara* workout today."

"I have your things ready." Helena gestured toward a neatly folded stack of white clothes on the counter. "Just in case."

"He's waiting for you outside." Sergey reached for a biscuit. "If you want to, of course."

Alexander hesitated, frowning. "Why didn't Father ask me himself last night?"

Sighing sadly, Helena shrugged. "Perhaps he didn't

29

want you to feel pressured. Or maybe he just didn't want to be around if you refused."

Alexander nodded. He had made a habit of rejecting most of Worf's attempts to teach him anything Klingon, but not this time. Knowing how rigorous his father's exercise routines could be, he'd probably be too tired to throw a temper tantrum for days.

Wearing a belted, white tunic and matching pants, Alexander joined his father on the lawn behind the house. Perhaps sensing that he was nervous, Worf instructed him in some basic loosening up exercises before launching into the intensive *Mok'bara* ritual.

"What happened to the green lamp that used to stand in the front foyer?" Worf asked casually as he rolled his head back and then from side to side. "Did your grandmother finally decide to get rid of it?"

"No." Alexander parroted his father's movements. "I finally broke it."

Worf did not even blink. "That was inevitable, I suppose."

"That's what Grandma said." Flexing his shoulders, Alexander tried not to smile. When Helena had found the smashed remains of the old lamp he had accidently knocked off the hall table, she had laughed. As a child, Worf had repeatedly bashed into and knocked it over, too. He just hadn't bashed into it so hard that it literally hurled itself to certain destruction on the floor.

"What did she say?" There was just a hint of anxiety in Worf's deep voice.

"That it was a miracle the lamp had survived one Klingon. Expecting it to survive two had been foolish."

Laughing, Worf straightened. "Your grandmother is a very wise woman."

Yes, she is, Alexander thought soberly. Knowing her adopted son and grandson better than they knew themselves, she had reunited them a second time. The dread he had felt before Worf disembarked at the shuttle terminal had been unfounded. There had been no punishment for the incident with Howard Chupek, only understanding. Maybe the gap separating him and his father wasn't as big as he had thought.

Finishing his warm-up, Worf suddenly grew serious. "The *Mok'bara* is one of the most effective disciplines young Klingons use to control the violence of adolescence. *If* they want to control it."

Alexander frowned suspiciously. "Meaning a lot of Klingons would rather fight?"

"It is in our nature and difficult to resist."

"That's *not* what you said yesterday," Alexander countered hotly. "You said—"

"I remember what I said." Worf sharply cut him off. "When I was at the Boreth Monastery after the *Enterprise* was destroyed at Veridian Three, Master Lourn tried to convince me that our violent Klingon nature could not be conquered, that Klingons will deliberately create conflict when there is none because of our innate aggressive tendencies. I *know* that is not true. Klingons can rise above their instincts—if they want to."

Alexander crossed his arms and cocked his head, challenging the statement. "For sure?"

"I did, eventually." Worf frowned slightly, but the fleeting shadow of pain in his eyes quickly vanished. "Discovering the *Mok'bara* helped. If I had sent you to a Klingon school when you first came to the *Enterprise,* you would have learned these techniques years ago."

"Maybe, but I'm glad I stayed with you instead." Alexander shrugged. He had never been interested in learning the martial arts discipline of *Mok'bara* before. It was so . . . Klingon. Now, he was desperate enough to try anything. He didn't quite believe that a ritual designed to hone combat skills could help him *control* the urge to fight, but Worf was so certain that he decided to give it a shot.

"I am glad you stayed, too. But it appears I did not teach you many of the things you need to know. For instance, there is no honor in attacking those weaker than yourself because you can not leash your anger."

"Howard Chupek insulted your father!" Seething, Alexander gritted his teeth.

"But there were other ways to handle the situation," Worf said patiently. "Fighting to settle grievances is acceptable in Klingon society. It is not acceptable here. I should have anticipated your current problem and taken measures to prepare you to cope with it."

"You tried," Alexander said honestly, relieved as the surge of anger subsided. "I wouldn't cooperate."

"That was then. This is now." Moving in front of the boy, Worf assumed a posc with his body bent slightly forward and his feet spaced wide apart. "Watch me and remember. When I stop, execute the movements as best you can."

Alexander anxiously studied his father's controlled stance and memorized the slow, deliberate motions of his hands and arms. When Worf paused, he tried to duplicate the exercise. His movements felt awkward and clumsy compared to the powerful grace his father displayed. Performing the Klingon ritual in the Rozhenkos' backyard on a bright, sunny morning only added to his sense of being totally out of place in his adopted world. The colorful flower gardens, fruit laden trees, stone

birdbaths and wooden climbing toys were hardly an appropriate setting for the intensive *Mok'bara.* For once, he was glad there were no close neighbors to spy on them.

"The form clears the mind," Worf said. He moved his hands forward, then brought them to an abrupt halt with a sharp intake of breath. "As the movements become ingrained, connecting your mind and body in a natural flow, you will feel more in control."

"I feel silly." Alexander instantly regretted the words and hastened to qualify the remark. "I mean, I used to pretend I was a Cossack fighting off European invaders in this yard. Don't Klingons do these ritual things in ancient caves with torches and stuff?"

Freezing in position, Worf slowly turned his head. "No. Obviously, I have neglected your Klingon education to a greater degree than I thought. However, we will address that at a later time. As far as the *Mok'bara* is concerned, it is a discipline of mind and body. Location is irrelevant."

"Oh. Sorry." Alexander watched attentively as his father resumed the exercise. If nothing else, Alexander told himself as he self-consciously executed an intricate pattern of quick thrusts and turns, maybe he'd learn to fight better. And that couldn't hurt. He was the only Klingon attending his school—one against three hundred.

After half an hour of grueling concentration, Worf relaxed and gestured toward a stone bench under a large shady tree. "That's enough for now."

Alexander nodded. He felt both drained and invigorated by the constant mental and physical tension inherent in the *Mok'bara* exercises. His own fitness routine utilized more energetic activities that strengthened muscles, agility and endurance without making such rigid demands on the mind. Still, he was in superb physical condition and the weariness surprised him. Rejecting it, he suddenly sprinted across the lawn toward the jungle gym his grandfather had built out of logs. Executing a high vault in a layout position with a half twist, he landed solidly without a misstep and raised his arms.

Worf roared with Klingon approval and shook his fist in the air.

Grinning, Alexander ran over and flopped down on the bench. Pouring two glasses of lemonade from the pitcher Helena had left on the side table, he handed one to his father.

"I did not know you had such a talent for gymnastics," Worf said. "Are you on the team at school?"

"No." Alexander frowned and shook his head. The question instantly darkened his mood as surely as a sudden storm cloud would have blotted out the sun.

"I am surprised the gymnastics coach has not insisted." Worf scowled. "An athlete with your abilities would ensure victory for the school's team."

"The coach doesn't know," Alexander mumbled. Besides, Jeremy Sullivan and Kim Ho *were* on the gymnastics team. They would not welcome a Klingon, no matter how well he performed.

Worf raised a more surprised eyebrow. "How can he not know? Do you not participate in gymnastics in physical education?"

"Yes. It's required." Alexander evaded the whole truth and shifted uncomfortably.

"But you do not perform as well as you could."

Alexander blinked, then nodded. His father's insight was astounding. It had been hard enough being the only one of his kind at school before the new Klingon-Federation conflict had started. Even then, he had quickly learned that showing off his superior prowess in sports was not the way to make friends. Flaunting his abilities now would just cause more trouble with his hostile classmates—and he already had more than he could handle. Jeremy Sullivan, Kim Ho and Bernard Umbaya were making sure of that.

"I often wish I had had the strength of character to overcome my competitive nature when I was your age. If I had been secure enough to hide my abilities . . ." Worf paused with a faraway look in his eyes.

"Huh?" Alexander squinted, totally puzzled. During their times together, Worf was always saying or doing something that caught him off guard. But his father had never paid him this ultimate compliment before. To his shame, his father's assumption was false. "I don't hold back because I have strength of character. I don't let anyone see what I can do because I'm a coward."

"You are many things, Alexander, but you are not a coward."

"Yes, I am." The confession hurt Alexander to the very core of his human-Klingon soul, but he had made a vow long ago never to lie to his father again. "I'm afraid all the kids will gang up on me."

"I see." Worf sighed. "Would you fight back to defend yourself?"

"Of course!" Alexander sat back indignantly. "But I'd probably lose."

"There are far more dishonorable things than losing an unfair fight."

"Like what?"

Worf sighed. "Like being so positive you are better at

something than everyone else, you cause a friend to die needlessly."

Alexander gasped. "You didn't do that. You couldn't have!"

"Not deliberately, no." Worf's eyes filled with sadness. "Your grandparents and I lived on the farm world of Gault for several years before coming here. I was captain of the school soccer team when I was thirteen. Because the score was tied in a game I desperately wanted to win, I pushed a teammate to intercept a play that was rightfully his. I shoved Michail so hard, he broke his neck and died the next day."

Speechless, Alexander just stared at his father's face. The intense pain was only evident in Worf's eyes.

Worf gripped Alexander's knee tightly. "That was when I realized that because I was bigger and stronger, I had to learn how to harness my aggressive nature. It is a lesson I do not want *you* to learn the hard way."

"Me neither," Alexander whispered, recalling how he had felt in the terminal. If his father hadn't stopped him, Howard Chupek would be in the hospital—or dead. "I'll learn control. I have to."

Worf nodded. "It will be a difficult task, especially if your friends are provoking you like Howard Chupek did."

"I can do it." Alexander eyed his father with grim determination. "And I promise I won't start another fight or break anything in a fit of temper ever again."

"That is not a promise you should make lightly, Alexander. I know how easy it is for the anger to take over." Another almost-smile played at the corner of Worf's mouth. "I remember one glass table on the *Enterprise* that was a particularly spectacular victim because I was frustrated and lost control. That was not the first time I failed to contain it and it may not be the last."

"My word of *honor!*" Alexander's eyes flashed. The oath was a bond stronger than any restraint or potential punishment and it was absolutely necessary to protect himself and those around him. Like his father and all Klingons, he would rather die than break his given word.

"For a week," Worf said gravely. "That is a reasonable goal and one you can achieve. You can renew your vow in seven days when we celebrate the Day of Honor."

"Okay. One week for starters."

"So be it." Rising, Worf set his glass down. "We have today and tomorrow before you return to school. I strongly suggest we accelerate your training with the *Mok'bara*. Then I will teach you some ancient meditations that have helped me."

Alexander followed his father back into the center of the lawn stricken with a deep sense of irony. Having denied his Klingon heritage for most of his young life, it was unsettling to find out that he *had* to acknowledge and accept his genetic inclinations in order to reject them. Without knowledge of his nature and proper training in Klingon methods, he would be fighting blind and unarmed with no way to win.

And sooner or later someone would get hurt—or worse.

CHAPTER 5

"Out of my way, lumphead!" Shoving Alexander aside, Bernard Umbaya laughed and kept walking down the crowded school hallway.

As Alexander stumbled backward against his locker, his PADD slipped out of his hand. When he leaned over to pick up the compact computer, a foot stomped down on it.

A Tellarite exchange student walking by snorted with jeering disgust. Two girls heading in the opposite direction giggled.

"Get off it!" Alexander snapped, then looked up into Jeremy Sullivan's scowling face.

Somehow, he had managed to avoid a direct confrontation with Jeremy and his friends during the previous two days. Using the *Mok'bara* mental skills his father had taught him, he had also managed to appear unaffected and in control when the other kids had shunned or insulted him. A lot of them had given up trying to provoke him. His faked indifference took the fun out of it. Jeremy was not so easily put off.

"Your PADD doesn't belong on the floor, Kling-on!" Blue eyes gleaming with arrogance, Jeremy lifted his foot, then kicked the PADD away when Alexander reached for it. The personal access display device shot across the corridor and banged against the far wall.

Alexander froze, silently counting to ten as he tried to confine the rage. His pulse and breathing quickened as he locked gazes with the red-haired boy. He kept counting, desperately wishing Jeremy would just move on before the rage won. But Jeremy didn't move and Kim Ho suddenly appeared beside him. Surrounded with his back against the wall, Alexander rose into a defensive posture, fists clenched at his sides.

"You don't scare me, Alexander." Jeremy leaned toward him, his voice low and intimidating. "Starfleet officers aren't afraid of Klingon dogs like you."

"We're not Starfleet officers, yet," Kim said with an uneasy glance at Alexander.

"But we will be." Jeremy's jaw flexed as his hateful gaze bore into Alexander.

Alexander stared back, his hard nails biting into the skin of his palms as he tightened his fists. One more word and Jeremy Sullivan would be heading toward the nurse's office with a broken jaw.

"Come on." Kim tugged on Jeremy's sleeve. "We're gonna be late."

Jeremy's cold gaze remained fastened on Alexander as Kim pulled him into the stream of students on their way to class. "Watch yourself, Klingon."

Feeling the rage begin to slip past his defenses, Alexander whirled and slammed his fist into the locker. Hearing a startled cry, he snapped his head around and gasped.

Brown eyes wide with anxious uncertainty, Suzanne Milton stood beside him clutching his PADD. She shoved it toward him. "You dropped this."

Swallowing hard, Alexander self-consciously took the PADD. Suzanne sat behind him in fundamental physics and he had become uncomfortably aware of her recently. She had long, flowing brown hair and freckles and he had often caught her watching him with guarded curiosity. Convinced that she would refuse any friendly overtures, he had not had the courage to start a conversation. Now that she was here, talking and being nice, he felt totally tongue-tied.

"Jeremy can be such a jerk." Suzanne smiled shyly.

"Thanks." Alexander smiled back and was appalled when the smile turned into a guttural snarl.

Drawing back with surprised indignation, Suzanne turned and walked away.

"I'm sorry. I . . ." Slumping against his locker, Alexander watched as she disappeared into a classroom. The bright, pretty girl was the only person in school who had been friendly toward him in weeks! He was sure she wouldn't make *that* mistake again. He had snarled in her face! No wonder humans despised Klingons.

Keying in his lock code, Alexander opened his locker and took out a data bar. He had had library authorization coded into the pass earlier. Although he could access any information he needed for his paper on thermal dynamics with his PADD, he preferred working in the library to being in regular study hall. The rows of computers and long, tall stacks of old-fashioned bound books provided a seclusion that wasn't possible in an open classroom.

As he trudged up the stairs to the second floor, Alexander was only vaguely aware of the sneers and whispered comments of the other students he passed. His anger at himself for growling at Suzanne was potentially more explosive than an anger directed at someone else. He imagined he was climbing a treacherous mountain, a mental exercise that kept his mind focused on his feet instead of on the disturbing incident with Suzanne.

"Hello, Alexander." The librarian, Ms. Marconi, smiled tightly as he handed her the pass. "How are you today?"

"Fine," Alexander mumbled. Before his Klingon temper had emerged to totally disrupt his life, he had liked the attractive librarian. Slim with shoulder-length blond hair and laughing green eyes, Ms. Marconi had always treated him with respect and kindness. But she wasn't fooling him with her pleasant attitude now. Last week he had almost smashed a computer screen when it failed to respond to a simple voice command. He had roared and kicked the sturdy desk instead. No permanent damage had been done, but the outburst had brought him dangerously close to being banned from the library for the rest of the semester. Ms. Marconi wasn't worried about him. She was worried about the safety of the library, its contents and the students in her charge.

"So. What's on your agenda this time?" Ms. Marconi ran the pass through a scanner to check the authorization, then gave it back.

"Physics." Jamming the data bar into his pocket,

Alexander nodded toward the towering shelves of bound books. "I want to look up a few things in the original texts."

"Oh." Ms. Marconi smiled, looking both relieved that he wouldn't be using the computers and nervous because he would be using the precious leather-bound books with paper pages. "Let me know if you have trouble finding anything."

"Okay." Alexander hurried away from the front desk and quickly found a table in a far corner. No one else was in sight. Grabbing a physics reference book off the shelf just in case Ms. Marconi came by to check on him, Alexander eased into the corner chair.

Concealed by high shelves lined with books of different sizes and colors, he settled down to work, hoping the hour would pass without interruption. He had only two classes after this. With luck, he'd get through another day without starting a fight or breaking something. There were only two more days to go until the *Batlh Jaj,* the Day of Honor, and his vow to his father remained unbroken.

Alexander was surprised at how much that meant to him. Thinking about it in the quiet solitude of the library, he realized that the significance of the *Batlh Jaj* went far beyond a holiday that celebrated the Klingons' unwavering dedication to honor. It was the oath itself. The belief that a person was only as trustworthy and strong as his given word was the one Klingon tradition he agreed with without reservation. It was the first lesson Worf had taught him on the *Enterprise.* More importantly, swearing to abide by it had been the first solid thread binding them together as father and son.

Honor bound.

He *would* rather suffer a horrible punishment than disgrace himself and his father by breaking his promise.

"I'm not kidding," a boy's voice insisted. "It's a first edition of Zefram Cochrane's *The Potential of Warp Propulsion* and it has a type error in it."

"They called that a typo." Kim corrected Bernard as they walked around the end of the long bookcase forming an aisle that ran along the back wall.

Sitting at the far end of the row, Alexander held his breath as Jeremy followed, looking bored.

"So what?" Jeremy asked.

"So he corrected and initialed it." Bernard scanned the upper shelves, looking for the volume.

"No, he didn't," Jeremy scoffed. "Some joker with a replicated pen initialed it so fools like you would *think* Zefram Cochrane did."

Kim noticed Alexander and tapped Jeremy on the shoulder.

Alexander stiffened, sensing that his oath was about to be tested. He reinforced the heavy, metal door imprisoning the imaginary lion in his mind with a huge padlock and several duranium bars. As long as the symbolic beast didn't get out, his very real rage wouldn't escape, either.

"Well, well. Look who's here." Jeremy sauntered down the aisle with Bernard and Kim close behind. They stationed themselves around the table, blocking Alexander's only way out. "What's a Klingon doing in a library?"

"My homework," Alexander said evenly.

"On what?" Bernard grinned and nudged Kim. "The

44

only thing Klingons are any good at is hunting and killing."

"Like the savages you are," Kim added. He wasn't smiling. "My uncle was killed in a Klingon raid near the Cardassian border."

"I'm sorry." Tense with the effort of caging his temper, Alexander knew he didn't sound as sincere as he felt. "But I didn't have anything to do with that."

"You're a Klingon, aren't you?" Eyes narrowed, Kim lunged toward the table with his fist raised. Jeremy, the undisputed leader of the trio, put a staying hand on Kim's chest. Bristling, Kim stepped back.

"I'm surprised Ms. Marconi let you back in after the fit you threw last week." Thumbing through the physics reference book on the table by Alexander's PADD, Jeremy frowned. "This is a Starfleet reference!"

Alexander didn't respond. The rage was gaining strength. The imaginary lion repeatedly threw itself at the metal door in his mind. The door boomed and bowed, snapping one of the duranium bars and cracking another. Closing his eyes, he mentally replaced the broken bar with a newer, stronger one. It broke almost instantly when Jeremy grabbed the front of his shirt.

"Are you spying for the Empire?"

"I am a Federation citizen." Alexander's lip curled in a snarl, revealing sharp canine teeth. His gaze was like a steel rod boring into Jeremy's eyes. "My father is a Starfleet officer."

"Right. And my father's an Orion pirate!" Jeremy talked tough and released his hold with a flourish, but Alexander didn't miss the flash of uncertainty on his face.

Lowering his gaze to stare at the edge of the table,

Alexander hoped Jeremy would take it as a sign of defeat and leave. What he really needed was to focus on something nonthreatening while he willed the fury into submission. Every muscle strained in the struggle to subdue an enemy far more dangerous than Jeremy Sullivan.

Falling for the ploy, Jeremy backed off.

Alexander continued to stare at the table, afraid to look up before the rage was completely gone.

"Ready?" Jeremy's quiet voice pierced Alexander's concentration. "One. Two . . ."

Too late Alexander realized that his tormentors had not left, but had only retreated to execute a more damaging plan. His gaze snapped up.

Standing behind the end section of the aisle book-cases, Jeremy, Bernard and Kim pushed the stack over on the count of three. The shelving unit wasn't tall enough to reach and crush their Klingon target, but it would hit the table, trapping him behind it.

A combination of fear and fury broke through all of Alexander's mental defenses. Shrieking, he vaulted over the table as the bookcase toppled and the three boys darted for cover. He was only a split-second short of jumping clear when the unit crashed, spilling books all over the floor. The top corner edge landed on his sleeve, pinning his shirt to the top of the table.

Snarling with frustration, Alexander yanked his arm and tore his shirt. The sound of ripping fabric calmed the rage, but that wouldn't help him now.

Ms. Marconi and several curious students rushed up to the fallen bookcase to stare at the mess and him. Jeremy, Bernard and Kim had disappeared. The librari-an looked like she was on the verge of tears in spite of her troubled frown, but Alexander didn't harbor any illusions about why she was upset. Her grief was for the dumped and battered books, not for the Klingon boy who was so obviously guilty of the crime. She showed no mercy.

"The principal's office, Alexander," Ms. Marconi said in a flat voice. She pointed toward the door. "Now."

CHAPTER 6

Alexander sat ramrod straight and as unmoving as stone, his eyes riveted on the bulletin board hanging on the wall across from him. He had not shifted position since arriving at the school office over an hour before. His grandmother had not been able to contact his father immediately after Mrs. Miyashi called, but Worf was on his way now. Alexander focused on the hard bench, welcoming the discomfort. It helped him imprison the fury aroused because he had been falsely and unjustly accused. It also distracted him from his anxiety over the impending and unavoidable conflict with his father.

The bell for the last period of the day rang.

Alexander watched the wall, bearing the disgusted sighs of the office personnel and the cloaked glances of students in stoical silence. There was nothing he could do to alter their distorted perceptions of him. No human understood the degree to which a Klingon valued his honor.

And in this, Alexander realized, he was truly Klingon.

He would not break his silence just as he had not broken his oath.

His only regret was that his father would not know the truth.

All eyes turned toward the door as Worf strode through it. Everyone but Alexander held their breath. Even dressed in a casual shirt, loose pants and boots with his long hair clipped at the base of his neck, his father was an imposing and impressive sight.

Resolved not to shame himself further in his father's eyes, Alexander kept his expression blank when Worf paused before him. Neither one said a word as he stood up and they approached the counter.

"You must be Alexander's father." Mrs. Miyashi's voice singsonged with a nervous lilt.

"Yes."

The single word spoken in a deep, commanding bass set the office clerk fluttering to the end of the counter. "I'm sure Mr. Houseman will see you immediately."

"That would be appreciated."

"Yes, of course. Right this way." Nodding vigorously, Mrs. Miyashi rushed to the principal's office to announce their arrival.

If he hadn't been in so much trouble, Alexander would have smiled. Aside from the fear all Klingons evoked because of their appearance and reputation, his father had a way of sounding intimidating even when that wasn't his intention. Few outside himself had ever experienced the unique sensitivity his father hid so well.

But I don't think I'm going to see that side of him today, Alexander thought as he followed Worf into Mr. Houseman's office.

Tall, muscular and a commanding personality himself, Mr. Houseman motioned for Alexander and Worf to sit in the chairs in front of his desk. "Thank you for coming so promptly, Lieutenant Commander. I regret having to call you in, but Alexander's unruly behavior seems to be getting worse."

"So I have heard."

Worf did not even glance in his direction and Alexander cringed inwardly, but like his father, his face revealed none of the emotions churning within. He was determined to conduct himself with dignity. Fixing his gaze directly ahead, he listened without fidgeting as the principal explained what had happened in the library.

"There was a similar, although less destructive incident last week," Mr. Houseman finished. "We did give him a warning."

Worf turned to address Alexander. "Is that true?"

"Yes," Alexander said, still staring at the wall. His father asked the question in a way that allowed him to answer honestly. "I kicked a desk and I was warned."

Worf nodded, eyeing him thoughtfully. "I find it very difficult to believe you would deliberately destroy a bookcase after you gave me your word."

Alexander didn't respond. It wasn't a question.

Hoping to head off a dispute, Mr. Houseman interjected. "No one else was in the vincinity, Mr. Worf."

Worf's brow furrowed for a long moment before he pressed Alexander. "Do you have anything to say?"

"No, sir." Alexander could not defend or clear himself without snitching on Jeremy, Bernard and Kim. And that was something he simply couldn't afford to do. They would launch a campaign of unbridled revenge and he did not trust his ability to cage the fury. It was growing too powerful and at a much faster rate than his progress with the *Mok'bara*.

The three arrogant and unsuspecting boys could not possibly survive an encounter with him.

He wouldn't survive the oppressive guilt, especially if he ignored a way to avoid a fatal confrontation to save himself. His father had killed someone accidently. Yet, as strong and confident as Worf was, even he couldn't exorcise the guilt that haunted him.

The bitter alternative was to let his father believe he had lost his temper in the library, toppled the bookcase and broken his promise.

Alexander swallowed a sigh. Suffering Worf's disappointment would hurt, but no one would die from it. Besides, his father would be returning to *Deep Space Nine* in a few more days. He had to live with Jeremy Sullivan.

And himself.

Growing anxious in the prolonged silence, Mr. Houseman cleared his throat. "I am not unsympathetic to the fact that things have become rather difficult for Alexander, given the recent hostilities and a general lack of understanding between our two cultures."

Giving no indication of his inner feelings, Worf turned back to the principal. "Unfortunately, that is quite true. However, Alexander's loyalties do not lie with the Klingon Empire."

"No, of course not." Mr. Houseman shifted uncomfortably, weighing his options. "But I can't let his actions go unpunished. A week of detention, beginning tomorrow. Since his last class has already started, you may as well take Alexander home now."

"Is that acceptable to you, Alexander?"

For the first time since entering the office, Alexander looked at his father. It seemed like an odd question, but nothing in Worf's eyes or expression gave him a clue as to why he had asked it. In the overall scope of things, that hardly seemed important. "Yes, sir."

"Then the matter is settled." Worf stood up.

"Not quite," Mr. Houseman added quickly. "If anything like this happens again, I'll have no choice but to expel Alexander from this school."

"Understood. Good day, Mr. Houseman." Worf deftly dismissed the principal and motioned Alexander out the door.

Even through his daze of despair, Alexander heard Mr. Houseman sigh with relief as they left his office.

When Worf pointed him toward the nearest exit, Alexander stopped. "I have to put my data bar in my locker. We're not allowed to take them out of the building."

"Very well."

As Alexander led the way through the deserted corridors, his anxiety increased. His father's unemotional calm was worse than the flustered displays of annoyance he had exhibited on the *Enterprise*. Worf had been completely out of his element when he first accepted the responsibility of fatherhood. In his confused and frightened innocence, Alexander had been able to reduce the noble Klingon to a state of sputtering, bewildered frustration when not even the High Council's decree of discommendation two years before had caused a ripple in Worf's veneer of proud poise. He knew because Counselor Deanna Troi had found his unusual effect on his father both fascinating and amusing.

Alexander wasn't fascinated or amused now. Worf's apparent unconcern was making him more nervous and upset than the furious lectures ever had. Why wasn't his father fuming with anger? The boy choked back a gasp of alarm. Maybe Worf didn't care enough about him anymore to *be* devastated and disappointed by his misbehavior!

"Here it is." Alexander paused in front of the locker, and froze, his worry about his father's feelings suspended for a moment.

Suzanne Milton was walking briskly toward them with her own data bar clutched in her hand. As she passed, she raised her chin and tossed her long hair over her shoulder. The deliberate snub hit Alexander like a bucket of ice water.

Worf frowned. "Is this how everyone treats you?"

"Mostly." Sighing, Alexander keyed in his lock code. Since it didn't seem possible to make his situation worse, he decided to confess all. "But Suzanne has a *real* reason. She was being nice and I *snarled* at her."

Stunned, Worf blinked, then leaned closer. "Snarled at her?"

"I didn't mean to insult her. It just happened. I still can't believe it." Shaking his head, Alexander pulled the data bar out of his pocket. He was prepared to accept whatever punishment his father had in store for him when they got home, but he wasn't prepared for what he saw when he looked back around. Worf was headed down the hall toward Suzanne.

Aghast, Alexander sagged against his locker and watched helplessly. If the girl's view of the hall hadn't been blocked by her open locker door, she probably would have run screaming in terror. However, Worf took her by surprise with a smile. She's probably too shocked to scream, Alexander thought miserably, wondering and yet not really wanting to know what his father was up to.

When Worf finished speaking, Suzanne nodded, then dashed to the side exit.

Closing the locker door, Alexander confronted his father when he returned. "Why did Suzanne run out of the building? What did you say to her!"

"She was excused early because she has a rehearsal for a dance recital," Worf said.

"Oh."

"And I explained that when a Klingon boy snarls at a girl, it is a compliment, an expression of—affection."

"What?" Alexander's mouth fell open. He couldn't deny that he liked Suzanne and wanted to be friends. But even if that happened, which didn't seem likely now, it was foolish to think a friendship could ever develop into something more when they got older. "But she's a girl! I mean, she's pretty and smart and—human."

"She seemed pleased."

"She did?" Alexander frowned uncertainly. He wasn't sure which was more confounding: Suzanne's attitude toward a complimentary Klingon snarl or his father's efforts to rectify the unintended misunderstanding.

Worf urged him toward the door. "Human females are unpredictable, almost without exception. And many of them are not as fragile as they look."

Human females aren't the only ones who are unpredictable, Alexander thought. His father was doing a pretty good job of throwing him completely off-guard, too.

CHAPTER 7

Late the next afternoon, Alexander watched the seconds flash by on the detention hall clock, but he wasn't watching the time. He was lost in puzzled thought. After returning home the day before, Worf's attitude of unruffled acceptance had not wavered. He had neither dictated a punishment nor said another word about the library incident. Even his grandmother had seemed perplexed.

Alexander was pretty sure the startling change in his father's attitude was not because he didn't care. If that were the case, Worf wouldn't have tried to correct the problem with Suzanne. It was also safe to assume that the Starfleet officer with the Klingon soul would not accept a dishonorable act in patient, unaffected silence.

Which, Alexander finally had to conclude, could only mean that somehow Worf *knew* he had not pushed over the bookcase, that his honor-bound promise not to break anything in a fit of temper was intact.

Alexander smiled as the significance of that sank in. Worf's belief, based solely on faith without supporting evidence, was a demonstration of the absolute trust he had always hoped to earn, but never honestly thought he could.

The only question that remained was why his father hadn't challenged Ms. Marconi's and Mr. Houseman's assumption that he was guilty, especially since Worf obviously thought he was innocent.

"That's all for today. You're free to go."

Alexander shook himself out of his reverie as Mr. Cunningham dismissed him, the only student in the classroom. He didn't care. Discovering how much his father trusted him was worth spending a whole semester in detention. However, it was only five days.

One down and four to go.

He didn't even mind having to stay late at school tomorrow on the *Batlh Jaj,* Alexander realized as he grabbed his PADD and ran for the door.

"Walk!" Mr. Cunningham smiled as Alexander skidded to a halt. "Please, Mr. Rozhenko."

"Yes, sir." Grinning, Alexander made a show of walking as fast as he could without breaking into a jog—until he burst through the doors to the outside. Leaping into the air, he laughed aloud. For the first time in a long time, he had actually had a good day.

Jeremy, Bernard and Kim had left him alone. Since they hadn't been hauled into the principal's office, they must have figured out that he hadn't accused them. Maybe that had made them reevaluate their unfair attitudes and tactics. More likely, they were just afraid he'd change his mind and tell if they continued to torment him. Either way, their absence had made it much easier for him to control the persistent rage. The twinges of annoyance he had felt during the day had quickly been suppressed.

On the other hand, *he* had avoided Suzanne. In spite of his father's impression, he wasn't at all sure her reaction to his unwitting display of Klingon affection had been positive. Maybe she had run out of the building because the very idea made her sick to her stomach. If so, he didn't want that terrible truth confirmed. It was enough to know that she knew he had not deliberately been rude.

Yep, Alexander thought happily. All things considered, it had been an extremely good day.

And it wasn't over yet.

Anxious to get home, Alexander walked toward the soccer field to take the shortcut through the woods on the far side. As part of their Day of Honor celebration tomorrow evening, he and his father were going to stage an Honor Combat for his grandparents. When one Klingon challenged the honor of another, they fought the *Suv'batlh* to decide whose honor would be preserved. It was similar to the medieval practice of trial by combat between knights in that a warrior's character and courage were thought to determine victory as much as his skill. Wielding *bat'leths* and wearing full Klingon armor, he and his father would battle it out in the backyard, hopefully to the delighted horror of the elderly Rozhenkos. Although Worf wouldn't admit it, he had never quite outgrown his own mischievous delight in trying to shake his adopted parents' unruffled acceptance of his "brutal" Klingon nature.

Eager to practice with his *bat'leth,* the traditional curved sword of honor, Alexander started to run. He didn't want to waste what was left of the warm, sunny afternoon. Halfway across the playing field, he realized he had made a gross tactical error.

Jeremy Sullivan darted from the edge of the forest onto the field in front of him. Bernard Umbaya and Kim Ho jumped out from behind the goals and raced toward him from the base lines.

Alexander's near-perfect day turned as sour as a bunch of rotting Argelian grapes.

The boys were launching an attack even though he had protected them—from the principal, detention and himself.

His initial dismay was instantly dragged under a rising tide of outrage. Even he had his limits, and it wouldn't take much to push him over the edge of reason into a ferocious, fighting madness.

Keeping a tight rein on the aggressive impulses, Alexander stood his ground as the boys slowed and stopped about five feet away.

"So what's the deal, Klingon?" Jeremy asked, regarding him warily.

"No deal," Alexander said shortly. He was only guessing that Jeremy was referring to his silence, but asking a question, even for clarification, would imply that he was uncertain and intimidated. He was neither.

"You don't expect us to believe you're going to take the blame for smashing that bookcase without trying to get back at us, are you?" Kim's eyes narrowed in a dark scowl.

"Believe what you want," Alexander countered.

"Don't play dumb with us, Alexander," Bernard snapped. "No self-respecting Klingon would let us off the hook."

"That's right. Don't you Klingons have this thing about defending your *ho-nor.*"

Bernard put a ridiculing emphasis on the word that made Alexander bristle. Still, he held his temper even as the tension in his muscles mounted and the impatient fury sparked. "You don't know anything about honor, Bernard."

"Maybe you don't, either." Jeremy took a daring step forward. "Maybe you didn't snitch because you knew *we'd* do something about it."

"I had reasons you don't understand." Gritting his teeth, Alexander fought the terrible, burning desire to rip the smug, challenging sneer off Jeremy's face.

"Because you're a coward!" Kim's chest heaved. "My uncle was killed by a bunch of no-good, rotten, Klingon cowards!" The angry boy charged.

Alexander staggered backward with the momentum as the smaller boy's body smashed into him. The power of unleashed Klingon adrenaline surged through him. Staying on his feet, he grabbed Kim's arm and easily freed himself from the boy's tackling grasp. Every cell in his Klingon body screamed for blood, urging him to yank the frail arm out of its socket. He tossed Kim aside instead.

Landing on his back with a thud and a *whooshing* grunt as the impact forced the air from his lungs, Kim lay without moving.

Time came to a screeching halt for Alexander. He stared at Kim, stricken as he recalled the soccer player who had died because Worf had been careless with his superior strength. That image was one hundred percent more effective than trying to cage an imaginary lion and the heat of Alexander's anger turned cold with dread.

Get up!

Moaning softly, Kim struggled into a sitting position and drew a long, deep breath.

Relieved and focused on the stunned boy, Alexander didn't see Jeremy and Bernard lunge at him until the last second. His reflexes engaged before the attack registered in his mind. Jumping back and to the side, he deflected the force of Jeremy's fist against his jaw and eluded Bernard's clumsy grasp.

The Klingon rage exploded from the depths of every gene, demanding its innate right to fight. Alexander mentally shoved the urge back as efficiently as he evaded Jeremy's second attempt to smash his face. He ducked the punch, then whipped around, freeing his leg from the arms Bernard wrapped around it.

Howling in frustration, Bernard rose into a crouch with his fists raised before him. Jeremy circled, trying to flank him.

Getting a second wind, Kim stood up and advanced with Jeremy and Bernard.

Sweat glistened on Alexander's brow from the dual exertion of controlling the rage within and fending off the boys' assault without seriously hurting anyone. Realistically, he knew he couldn't keep the fury blocked indefinitely. And even though it was three against one, if the Klingon fury got out, the fury would win.

But the price of his assured victory would be too high.

Retreat was not a maneuver any Klingon considered except as a last resort. And even though a fleeing Bird-of-Prey survived to fight again, many Klingon commanders preferred to die. For Alexander, retreat was the only option. He could bear being branded a coward. He could not bear inflicting a crippling injury or causing a death.

Hoping the implied threat would keep his attackers at bay, Alexander raised his hands in a defensive *Mok'bara* position and slowly moved back.

"Come on!" Jeremy screamed. "Fight! Fight!"

"Chicken!" Bernard ran forward, swinging wildly.

Kim didn't say anything. He just charged.

Still moving backward toward the school, Alexander deftly warded off the blows. He instantly recognized an opportunity to flip Bernard, but didn't take it. He had not been practicing the offensive aspects of the art long enough to guarantee precision control. One wrong move and Bernard could snap his neck.

Coming in from behind, Jeremy slammed himself into the back of Alexander's knees. Unprepared, Alexander went down. All three boys fell on him with fists flying.

While Jeremy, Bernard and Kim battered muscle and bruised bone, the denied rage stormed a Klingon-human mind that would not and did not surrender.

A fist clobbered him in the eye and another blow split his lip. The salty taste of his own blood amplified the rage, but Alexander did not fight back.

The pounding stopped suddenly as new voices mingled with the boys' shouted curses and insults.

"Stop this!" A man demanded. "Stop this now!"

"Enough, Bernard!" An authoritative female snapped. "Kim! Alexander!"

Breathing hard, Alexander watched as Mr. Cunningham pulled Jeremy away. Ms. Marconi stepped between him and Bernard, saving him from one last punch. Kim backed off on his own.

"You know," Mr. Cunningham said crossly as Alexander struggled to his feet. "I was really looking forward to getting home, but thanks to the four of you, we'll all be spending the rest of this beautiful day with Mr. Houseman."

"And I don't think *he's* going to be too happy about being stuck here, either." Standing with her hands on her hips, Ms. Marconi glared at all four boys.

"He started it!" Bernard pointed to Alexander. Jeremy and Kim, looking suitably ashamed, nodded in agreement.

The librarian's incensed gaze shifted to fix on Alexander's dirt-streaked face. "How could you? Especially after Mr. Houseman gave you another chance."

"I did not start it." Alexander said, wondering if the slight narrowing of Ms. Marconi's eyes indicated disgust or uncertainty.

"Everything was fine when you left detention, Alexander." Either disregarding or not hearing Alexander's denial, the science teacher threw up his hands in exasperation. "What could these three possibly have done that was worth starting a fight and getting thrown out of school?"

I was ambushed, Alexander thought. He would have said so if he thought anyone would listen. He seriously doubted anyone would. Sighing he fell into step beside Jeremy as Mr. Cunningham marched them back to the building and the principal's office.

"Gotcha, Klingon," Jeremy whispered. "You're out of here."

Alexander didn't give the gloating boy the satisfaction of a response. The disgrace of being expelled would pass someday, but if he couldn't convince his father he had not started the fight, the breach of faith between them might never be healed.

Who would Worf believe?

A rebellious son who had challenged his ideals and brought him more trouble than joy over the years?

Or everyone else?

CHAPTER 8

Sitting on the hard bench in the school office, Alexander stared at the three boys perched on chairs across from him. With an expression of inscrutable indifference frozen on his face, he did not blink, twitch, or in any way react to their whispered discussion. The cut on his lip stung and his blossoming black eye throbbed. He ignored those irritations, too.

Behind the counter, Mrs. Miyashi watched all of them like a hawk, ready to sound the alarm at the first hint of trouble. Mr. Houseman was still in his office. Jeremy's father and Bernard and Kim's mothers had already arrived and were waiting in the conference room with Mr. Cunningham and Ms. Marconi. Alexander didn't know when his father would show. Worf had gone to Starfleet Headquarters to attend a research and development briefing about new security technologies. Alexander was sure he would not leave before the presentation was finished.

A buzzer sounded on Mrs. Miyashi's desk. Rising, she

headed for the principal's office and paused at the door to glance at her charges. "Nobody moves. Do I make myself clear?"

The human boys nodded.

"Yes." Alexander answered without moving anything except his mouth. The instant Mrs. Miyashi closed the door behind her, the boys fastened their intent, triumphant eyes on him.

"Defeat is as bitter as they say, isn't it, Alexander?" Jeremy smiled.

"And victory is sweet." Bernard nodded emphatically. "We'll probably get a month of detention, but you know? It's worth it to get rid of you."

Kim just stared back.

Remembering how devastated he had been when his mother died, Alexander sympathized. But unlike Kim, who had targeted the entire Klingon race because he did not know the face or the fate of his uncle's killer, he knew a certain, painful peace. Duras would never kill again. His father had risked his Starfleet career to claim the right of revenge under Klingon law and had killed the murdering traitor. Kim had no such comfort and Alexander sincerely wished there was some way he could diffuse the emotional time bomb the boy was carrying around.

"We won our war against you, Alexander." Jeremy leaned forward to drive his point home. "And Starfleet will win against the Klingon Empire, too."

"But," Worf's deep voice boomed from the doorway. "It would be more beneficial for all concerned if our differences could be settled peacefully."

As though operating as a single unit, all three boys gasped. Eyes widened and jaws fell open as Lieutenant

Commander Worf, wearing his red and black Starfleet uniform and a silver Klingon sash, stepped into the room.

"You really are a Starfleet officer!" Jeremy stated the obvious in a hushed rasp. "How can that be?"

"I graduated from Starfleet Academy." Worf spoke without a hint of humor and dismissed the stunned boy by simply looking away.

Alexander tried not to smile. It was a struggle easily won when he saw the hard gleam in his father's gaze when their eyes met.

Mrs. Miyashi's hand clamped to her chest as she left Mr. Houseman's office and spotted the towering Klingon standing by the counter. "We've been waiting for you to arrive, Mr. Worf. If you'll just have a seat in the conference room with the other parents—"

"You and they will have to wait a while longer," Worf said bluntly. He was not asking permission.

"Oh, uh . . . really?" Mrs. Miyashi swallowed hard.

"I will discuss this matter with my son first. In private."

Alexander's heart lurched.

Jeremy and Bernard couldn't stop staring.

Kim frowned.

Stricken mute, Mrs. Miyashi pointed to the door leading into the guidance counselor's office.

With a curt nod, Worf turned toward the indicated door. "Come with me, Alexander."

Breathing in deeply, but keeping his own impassive expression fixed, Alexander stood up and followed his father. He did not acknowledge the four pairs of eyes that followed him.

"Sit down." Motioning toward one of two chairs by an uncluttered desk, Worf closed the office door.

Alexander sat, bracing himself for the worst as Worf sank into the other chair.

"Have you been falsely accused again, Alexander?"

Alexander had expected his father to be direct, but he had not anticipated the question asked. He answered in stammering awe. "Uh . . . yes."

"I see." Worf lapsed into thoughtful silence a moment before continuing. "Did these same boys push over the bookcase in the library yesterday?"

Alexander could only nod, astounded yet again by his father's blind belief that he had kept his given word. The questions Worf asked did not challenge his honesty, but merely sought additional information.

"Why did you not say so when we were in Mr. Houseman's office?"

Shrugging, Alexander explained. "Everyone was so sure I did it, I didn't think anyone would believe me."

Worf frowned. "That is not sufficient reason to take the blame and accept punishment for something you did not do."

"No." Alexander paused, but he didn't even consider trying to hide the truth. "I thought that if I told, Jeremy and Bernard and Kim would try to get back at me. I wasn't afraid of a fight," he added quickly. "I just wasn't sure I'd be able to . . . control myself if I got into one."

"You did not want to risk hurting or . . . killing anyone."

Alexander shook his head. "No."

"But they attacked you anyway."

"Yeah. They wanted to get me before I got them, except I wasn't even *thinking* about getting revenge."

Nodding, Worf gently touched the dried blood on Alexander's lip, then glanced at the closed door. "They

do not appear to have any broken bones, bruises or black eyes."

"I could have torn them apart with my bare hands!" Alexander's eyes flashed with Klingon fire, then he exhaled in self-disgust. "But I didn't fight back. I *am* a rotten Klingon just like Kim said. Just not for the reasons he thinks."

"I was not aware that you *wanted* to be Klingon." Worf blinked, unable to hide his surprise.

"I don't. Not exactly." Alexander shifted position and averted his gaze. "I want to be like you."

Worf just stared at him.

Misinterpreting the long silence that followed, Alexander tried to cover the admission he had not intended to voice. "I wanted to make you proud, not ashamed."

"Ashamed?" Worf started. "I am *not* ashamed of you and *you* are not a . . . rotten Klingon. Your ability to control your temper under such trying circumstances is impressive. And there is no dishonor in not fighting back when the decision is made in the interest of a greater good."

"There isn't?" Alexander looked up with a puzzled frown.

"No. After I avenged K'Ehleyr by killing Duras, I made a decision *not* to challenge the High Council to clear our family's name for the good of the Empire."

"But Duras's father betrayed Khitomer to the Romulans, not Mogh!"

Worf sighed. "That is true, but the entire High Council had supported the lie and shared the dishonor that went with it. To expose them would have thrown the Empire into chaos."

Alexander raised an eyebrow. "But that happened anyway."

"Yes." Worf sighed. "When the Duras family challenged Gowron's right to lead the High Council, the result was civil war. My silence only delayed the inevitable."

"Yeah." Alexander nodded. "Now I wish I had defended myself about the bookcase, too. But it's too late now."

Worf sat back with a frown. "My decision bought Gowron valuable time. Taking the blame for the bookcase to avoid a potentially dangerous confrontation was a wise decision as well."

"Except it didn't work!" The heat of anger warmed Alexander's blood, but the heat quickly dissipated in the cold of bitter despair. "There was still a fight and everyone thinks I started it. Just like everyone thinks I dumped that bookcase. Even if I told the truth, no one would believe me now."

"Truth does not stay buried forever," Worf said. "The Duras lie was exposed and our honor *was* restored by Gowron when he emerged victorious in the civil war."

"Yeah, but then Gowron kicked us out of the Empire again."

"Yes." Worf's jaw flexed with tension. "He wanted me to join him when the Empire broke the alliance with the Federation. I chose to remain in Starfleet. He did not understand that being truly Klingon, my oath of allegiance to the Federation was just as binding as if I had sworn to be loyal to him."

Alexander couldn't help but notice the fleeting sadness that clouded his father's eyes. Gowron had robbed them of their place on the High Council, their lands and their titles and evicted them from the Klingon Empire. Worf had even lost his brother, whose memories had been erased and replaced with a new identity to save him. Not only did Kurn no longer remember Worf as his brother, he despised and reviled him.

Now, Alexander realized with a profound sadness he had not felt before, all they had left of their Klingon heritage was each other and their honor—which Worf had never compromised.

"However, that is beside the point," Worf continued. "Gowron *had* to set aside my discommendation because his honor would not allow him to ignore the truth about Mogh's loyalty to the Empire at Khitomer. And I believe that someday he will pay highly for dismissing my oath to the Federation as irrelevant. Honor does prevail."

"When you're dealing with Klingons," Alexander pointed out. "My word doesn't mean anything here because these people don't understand the importance of a Klingon's oath. None of what's happened is my fault, but I'm going to be expelled anyway."

Worf bristled. "I will not allow them to expel you for something you did not do."

Alexander appreciated that, but his father's perspective had been distorted by his years in Starfleet. Because Starfleet incorporated so many different races and species, tolerance and understanding of alien cultures was imperative. With the exception of himself and an occasional exchange student from another world, the school's teachers and students had never had to take critical cultural differences into consideration.

"I don't think you can stop them," Alexander said honestly. "It's my word against the word of three humans who lie."

Worf's eyes narrowed thoughtfully. "By lying, those

boys have challenged your honor. Consequently, they may also have provided us with the means to solve both your problems."

"Both problems?"

"This school's lack of knowledge about Klingon culture and the false accusation. There is a way, but you must trust me without question."

How? Alexander wondered, his mind racing with a dozen more questions. He did not ask them.

"You have my word," Alexander said solemnly.

CHAPTER 9

As Alexander took his place back on the bench, Worf looked at all four boys in turn, then addressed Mrs. Miyashi. "They will remain here until called. I must speak to their teachers and parents alone."

"Uh, well. If it's all right with Mr. Houseman, I suppose—"

"If what's all right?" Mr. Houseman frowned as he stepped out of his office.

"I will explain in the conference room, Mr. Houseman." Without giving the principal a chance to reply or argue, Worf opened the conference room door and strode inside. He stopped at the near end of the long table. All five humans seated around it reacted to his entrance with varying degrees of alarm and curiosity.

Mr. Houseman followed, remaining calm and collected as he walked past Worf and sat down at the head of the table. "Please, Mr. Worf. Have a seat."

"Thank you. I will stand."

"You're not on trial here, Mr. Worf," the principal assured him kindly.

"No, but Alexander is and I am convinced he has been falsely accused—for the second time in two days." Worf had never understood the human tendency to "beat around the bush" and chose to get directly to the point. It was more efficient and gave him an immediate insight into the attitudes of the other people in the room.

He noted that the two women and one man seated to his left took exception to his statement. The dark-skinned woman frowned, but with consideration for his blunt declaration. The guarded stares of the woman of Asian descent and the man transformed into hostile glares. They were, he surmised, the other boys' parents. The pretty, blond woman on his right looked startled, then deeply troubled, suggesting she might agree. The man to her right appeared to be thoughtfully reserving judgment.

Mr. Houseman quickly introduced everyone. Nods were exchanged instead of handshakes, providing Worf with more helpful information. Mrs. Umbaya, the librarian and the science teacher greeted him with tight, hesitant smiles, indicating they were willing to listen. Mr. Sullivan and Mrs. Ho would be difficult to convince.

"The matter of the library bookcase is closed, Mr. Worf," Mr. Houseman said evenly. "We're here today because Alexander, Jeremy, Bernard and Kim were caught fighting on school property."

"Today's fight is a direct result of Alexander's silence concerning the bookcase." Worf also kept his voice even. "He did not defend himself yesterday because he mistakenly thought that taking the blame would *prevent* a confrontation. He did not start the fight."

"Are you saying that our kids did?" Mr. Sullivan demanded hotly.

"But why would they?" Mrs. Umbaya asked, genuinely puzzled.

Mrs. Ho shifted uncomfortably, but didn't speak.

Worf was not unsympathetic to their distress. He had not forgotten how embarrassed he had been when Ms. Kyle, Alexander's first teacher on the *Enterprise,* had informed him of his son's disturbing behavior in class. However, although he was determined to clear Alexander, he was more concerned with correcting the circumstances that had prompted the incidents than he was with seeing the other boys punished.

"As concerned and responsible parents, the question we must address is not who did what, but why—as Mrs. Umbaya asked a moment ago."

Mrs. Umbaya nodded, pleased with Worf's recognition.

"We are all aware that Klingons are savagely aggressive," Mr. Sullivan huffed. "Obviously, Mr. Worf's son must have done *something* to antagonize the others."

"Obviously?" Ms. Marconi glared at Jeremy's father. "Are all people of Irish descent alcoholics and terrorists?"

"Of course not!" Mr. Sullivan snapped, then blinked. A flush of humiliation crept up his neck as he cleared his throat. "Although, a few hundred years ago there were a lot of people who thought so. My deepest apologies for my prejudicial remark, Lieutenant Commander."

Worf accepted with a gracious nod.

"Prejudice." Mr. Cunningham sighed. "Humans have lived together without caring about our differences for so long, I didn't recogize the ugly beast when it was staring me in the face. Prejudice is the problem, isn't it, Mr. Worf?"

"I believe so." Worf scanned the troubled faces before him, noting that everyone but Mrs. Ho now seemed open to discussion. "In spite of the long alliance between the Federation and the Empire, Earth knows very little about our culture and values. Ignorance breeds misunderstanding."

"That doesn't change the fact that your son went berserk in the library yesterday!" An anger completely out of proportion to the circumstances twisted Mrs. Ho's face and flared in her eyes. *That* was no misunderstanding. Kim told me that Ms. Marconi caught Alexander red-handed."

"Actually—" The librarian sheepishly glanced at Mr. Houseman and then at Worf. "I didn't *see* Alexander push the case. His sleeve was caught between the bookcase and the table and he was the only one there when I arrived. But . . ."

"Yes?" Worf prodded.

Ms. Marconi sighed deeply. "Jeremy, Bernard and Kim were in the library at the time, too."

Mr. Houseman started. "And you think it's possible they did it?"

Ms. Marconi shrugged. "Possible, yes. But I can't prove it. Not unless they confess."

"The same is true of the fight today," Mr. Cunningham added. "Bernard *said* Alexander started it and the other two agreed, but we don't know that for a fact."

Appalled, Mrs. Umbaya gasped. "I can't believe Bernard would lie or do any of these terrible things just because Alexander is a Klingon."

"Kim would." Tears flowed freely down Mrs. Ho's cheeks. "My brother was killed by Klingons."

No one spoke for several seconds.

"I hate to admit it," Mr. Sullivan said softly, breaking the anguished silence, "but Jeremy could be guilty, too. He's been set on a Starfleet career since he was six years old. According to him, Bernard and Kim share his dream. Perhaps, in their youthful enthusiasm, they've forgotten that the primary function of Starfleet is exploration. The dispute with the Empire *has* put an unusual emphasis on combat."

"And Alexander is the face of the enemy." Exhaling, Mrs. Umbaya lowered her gaze.

"I'm at a loss how to proceed," the principal admitted, running his hand through his hair. "Without proof or confessions, we may never know what really happened in the library. However, I'm no longer *convinced* Alexander is guilty. Even so, they were all caught fighting on school grounds. I don't see any option but to punish all of them."

"I have a better idea." When everyone turned to regard him attentively, Worf plunged ahead. "The boys are the only ones who know the truth. It cannot be forced out of them, but must be offered willingly, as a matter of honor. Honor is not a concept unique to Klingons. It has been valued as a measure of an individual human's worth throughout your history. It is absolutely essential in Starfleet officers."

"Go on, Mr. Worf," Mr. Sullivan urged with a smile.

Alexander stood with Jeremy, Bernard and Kim at the edge of the table. The adults sitting around it watched them with expressions so grim and foreboding, he wondered if his father had been giving them lessons. He aimed his own gaze straight ahead, but he was aware of

Worf standing off to the side. His father's narrowed, piercing stare and proud stance were unmistakeable signs that he had shifted into pure Klingon-mode.

"Alexander!" Worf barked sharply.

Jeremy, Bernard and Kim flinched.

"Yes, sir." Swallowing hard, Alexander tried to bear in mind that his father had a plan. No matter what happened, he had to trust him—blindly and without question.

"Did you knock over the bookcase in the library?"

"No, sir. I did not."

"Do you know who did?"

"Yes."

Arms crossed over his massive chest, Worf strode forward and stopped before him. "Name them."

Alexander felt Jeremy tense beside him and hesitated. He wasn't sure what response his father expected. An honest and honorable one, he realized. "No."

Worf paused, tightening the tension with his silence. "That is your right. However, Bernard Umbaya *has* accused you of starting the fight on the soccer field."

Bernard sucked in his breath with a soft cry of alarm.

Mrs. Umbaya's hand quickly covered her mouth, but Alexander couldn't tell if she was hiding a smile or a gasp of horror.

Worf's attention remained riveted on him. "Did you?"

"No, sir."

Still speaking to Alexander, but moving so he faced Bernard, Worf spoke in a low, threatening tone. "Then *he* has insulted your honor."

"Yes."

"And tomorrow is the *Batlh Jaj!*"

Turning pale, Bernard jumped and looked imploringly at his mother. "Mom?"

Her only response was an unsympathetic scowl.

"*Batlh Jaj,*" Worf repeated slowly.

Alexander frowned. Was he supposed to say something?

"The Klingon Day of Honor," Worf said with a prodding look at Alexander. "The only day non-Klingons are allowed to participate in—"

"The *Suv'batlh!*" Shouting the word, Alexander suddenly realized what his father was trying to set up. Donning his most ferocious Klingon face, he turned to confront Bernard and snarled softly. "Because you've accused me with a lie, I challenge you to fight the Honor Combat."

"Combat?" Bernard squeaked.

Worf moved back, allowing Alexander to look each boy in the eye as he moved from one to the next. Normally, the *Suv'batlh* was fought three on three. Alexander had no companions to stand by him and decided to even up the odds.

"Three on one."

"Uh . . ." Desperate, Bernard looked at Jeremy, then Kim.

"We accept." Kim's eyes filled with his poisonous hatred.

"We do?" Bernard blinked uncertainly, then shrugged. "Right. We do."

"Gladly." Jeremy smiled with smug confidence.

Moving in again, Worf addressed Bernard. "Although the *Suv'batlh* traditionally takes place in the territory of the one whose honor has been challenged, this battle will be held on neutral ground. The school gym. Tomorrow morning. *Qapla!*"

Turning abruptly, Worf strode boldly out the door.

Alexander hesitated, then caught Ms. Marconi waving under the table for him to go, too. Holding his head up, he marched boldly after his father.

Worf did not alter the speed or cadence of his pace until they were outside and striding across the soccer field. Even then, Alexander had to jog to keep up.

"How did you get Mr. Houseman and the other parents to agree to a *Suv'batlh?*"

"Honor is just as important to most humans as it is to Klingons," Worf explained, deliberately slowing so Alexander didn't have to run. "They just do not advertise it as loudly or constantly as Klingons do."

"Oh." Alexander walked, feeling as darkly troubled as the twilight sky. "There's just one thing that bothers me about this whole thing, though."

"And that is?"

"Jeremy, Bernard and Kim don't know the first thing about using a *bat'leth* and I've been practicing for years. Fighting an Honor Combat with such an overwhelming advantage just doesn't seem fair."

Worf nodded. "An honorable observation. However, I assure you, tomorrow's *Suv'batlh* will be fairer to your opponents than they have been to you."

Bursting with curiosity, Alexander had to ask. "How can you be so sure?"

"Because . . ." Worf paused on the edge of the forest to look down on him. "The choice of weapons is yours."

CHAPTER 10

Standing by a fold-out screen positioned center stage just off the back wall, Alexander watched as the school gym was transformed for the Day of Honor assembly. If this had been a large school in a metropolitan area, the setting and props could have been programmed into the hologym, but the small Mirnee Doleena school was not equipped with that technological luxury. Worf, Ms. Petrovna and Mr. Santiago, the physical education teachers who had volunteered to help, were setting up the Klingon props his father and grandmother had taken out of storage or replicated the night before.

The gymnastics equipment had been relocated in the far half of the gym to make room for the *Batlh Jaj* presentation. The bleachers along both sides had been lowered to accommodate the students and teachers and chairs had been set in front of the tiers for Mr. Houseman, nonteaching personnel, his three opponents and their parents.

Ms. Petrovna and Mr. Santiago came into view push-

ing two metal *bat'leth* racks. After placing the racks a
few feet to each side of the screen, they hurried out
again.

Bustling with energy, Helena and Sergey Rozhenko
attached a large Klingon banner to the front of the
screen.

"What do you think, Alexander?" his grandmother
asked, her eyes bright with enthusiasm. "I made it for
your father a long time ago."

Alexander cocked his head, studying the red banner
with the symbol of the Empire emblazoned in gold at
the center. "It looks great. Very . . . Klingon."

"So do you!" Sergey beamed as he gave Alexander an
appreciative once-over. "You look quite . . . terrifying."

"Just like a warrior," Helena declared with proud
delight.

Alexander rolled his eyes, but the intended compli-
ments pleased him. Although the fitted black pants and
knee-high boots were comfortable, the belted, plated-
metal armor he wore over a black shirt felt awkward.
The buckled, metal-studded leather combat gloves
itched. He fought the urge to brush back his long hair,
which had been teased into a wild disarray that cascaded
over his shoulders. Still, he was glad to know his
appearance was intimidating. However, he doubted that
he looked nearly as fierce as his father.

"Your *bat'leth,* Alexander." Also dressed in the armor
of a Klingon warrior, Worf strode toward the small
group. Placing the ancient family *bat'leth* on the taller
rack, Worf handed another traditional sword to his son.
Alexander carefully put it on the shorter metal rack.
"Where are Ms. Marconi and Mr. Cunningham?"

"Right here!" Wearing a long Klingon robe made of
large blue, silver and brown patches over a black shirt

and pants secured with a wide, silver belt, the science teacher hurried across the gym floor. Ms. Marconi moved at a more sedate pace, looking regal in a similar robe of patched greens and golds worn over a long black dress belted in gold. Both of their faces shone with an eager excitement.

"So!" Mr. Cunningham clapped his hands together, obviously thrilled to be actively participating in the *Batlh Jaj* ceremony. "What do you want us to do?"

Waving Mr. Santiago over, Worf took a tall standard from the gym teacher's hands. The pole was fitted with metal balls alternated with curved and spiked, metal Klingon symbols. Then he pointed to one side of the screen. "You will stand here."

The teacher obediently stepped into the spot Worf indicated.

"Ordinarily," Worf said, "there are specific moments during the ritual when the standard bearer makes the staff sing." Small metal plates attached to chains hanging from the curved pieces jangled as Worf gently shook the pole. "However, since we do not have time for instruction, you may jangle at your discretion." He handed the standard to the teacher and turned away.

The science teacher hesitated, then shook the pole.

The plates jingled, drawing Worf's attention back.

Mr. Cunningham shrugged with a mischievous twinkle in his eye. "Just practicing."

Alexander smiled as his father left to get the remaining props. He was pretty sure the Klingon Empire would not approve of including non-Klingons quite so liberally in the ceremonial proceedings. His father's willingness to deviate from acceptable Klingon tradition was encouraging, though. If Worf could be this flexible, maybe their human audience would be, too.

"What about me?" Ms. Marconi looked at Worf expectantly when he returned.

"You will light the torches." Worf handed her a small, tech-torch. The tip would burst into flame when she pressed a button on the long shaft.

Ms. Petrovna and Mr. Santiago came back on stage pushing two more racks, each mounted with three unlit torches made of wood and pitch.

Worf caught Alexander's questioning glance as the gym teachers rolled the racks into position behind the *bat'leth* stands. "Under the circumstances, torches seemed . . . appropriate."

Alexander held up his hands, indicating he wasn't going to argue the point.

"It's almost time, Mr. Worf," Mr. Santiago said. "I just hope I don't miss my cues."

"The lighting is only for dramatic effect," Worf assured him with another glance at Alexander. "Part of the *stuff* so many people seem to associate with Klingon rituals. We are, after all, striving to make a symbolic point."

"I think everyone will be impressed." Giving Worf a thumbs-up, Ms. Petrovna followed Mr. Santiago to the far side of the gym.

After giving Alexander a supportive pat on the back, his grandmother went to join his grandfather on the chairs in front of the bleachers. Clasping the tech-torch in both hands, Ms. Marconi moved to center stage between the *bat'leth* racks. Taking a deep breath, Alexander followed Worf to wait behind the screen.

Seated behind the technical control board, Mr. Santiago opaqued the windows, throwing the gym into total darkness. A minute later, leaving the *Batlh Jaj* stage darkened, he raised the lights in the rest of the gym to a dim, twilight glow.

Alexander listened to the faint whisper of his father's breath and the muffled sounds of students and teachers filing in and finding seats. He could almost hear the pounding of his own anxious heart as it throbbed against his ribs. Heat flowed from the pulsing muscles into his blood in anticipation of the battle soon to be waged and the honor soon to be avenged. It coursed through major arteries, spreading to smaller ones, infusing every muscle and nerve with the raw power of being Klingon.

Alexander trembled as the intensity of the moment triggered a memory buried in the depths of his mind. The image of a familiar, aging Klingon face suddenly appeared.

K'mtar.

The trusted family advisor had arrived to prevent Worf's assassination at a *Kot'baval* festival on a remote Klingon outpost not long before the *Enterprise* had been destroyed. K'mtar had tried to force him into becoming a warrior with as much, if not more, fervent determination than his father. He had resisted, just as stubbornly as he had always rejected Worf's attempts. Then, without even saying good-bye, K'mtar had vanished from his life—and his thoughts.

Remembering now, Alexander was once again reminded of the irony inherent in his present circumstances. He had not consciously realized that Worf had stopped pressuring him to learn Klingon ways following K'mtar's departure. Their time together had been too short afterward. The destruction of the *Enterprise* had brought him back to Earth and sent his father to serve on *Deep Space Nine*. But even on his return, knowing his son's ignorance of Klingon control methods was partially responsible for his fits of violent temper, Worf had not pressed him. His father had only suggested. And finally, left to decide for himself, Alexander had agreed to explore the power of the Klingon self he had always denied.

But, Alexander realized in amazement, that power did not have a will of its own. Focusing his thoughts, he kept the fire from running wild, banked it to be called upon and used when and as he directed. Or so he hoped. He would not know if he was still a slave to the savage in his genes or if he had tamed it until the *Suv'batlh* began.

The lights dimmed to near darkness and Worf tensed beside him.

The hiss and crackle of Ms. Marconi's tech-torch bursting into flame and the audience's collected gasp of hushed awe touched Alexander's ears. He watched his father as the librarian lit the wooden torches on their right and left. When Worf turned to signal him that it was time to begin, their gazes locked for a long moment. He could sense the tension mounting in the crowd waiting for whatever happened next. His own nerves were taut with excitement. Then, returning Worf's nod, he moved around the right end of the screen as his father moved to the left.

Matching his father's movements, Alexander paused before the rack of burning torches on his side of the stage. Ms. Marconi stood in front of the Klingon banner, still clutching her torch. A subtle scowl of Klingon contempt was fixed on her pretty face. Mr. Cunningham waited on his right, holding the standard steady and

silent, looking impressively superior and composed. Which, Alexander reflected, wasn't all that difficult for a teacher.

Their dramatic appearance had the desired effect, though. More gasps and anxious whispers rippled through the assembly. The audience's undivided attention had been captured as surely as a shuttle snagged in a starship's tractor beam.

"Batlh Jaj!" Worf's booming voice roared. A spotlight suddenly illuminated his head and upper body, augmenting the flickering light from the torches.

"The Day of Honor!" Alexander translated loudly as a flash of light enveloped him, too.

Mr. Cunningham jangled.

Perfect! Tensing, Alexander listened as his father recited a brief explanation of the holiday's origin in sharp, staccato Klingon.

"Jatlh ta' tlhIngan Du yuQ! Nob'ta Wo' che—"

Mesmerized by the power of Worf's commanding voice, no one stirred in the darkness even though they didn't understand a word. Alexander wouldn't have understood, either, except that he had memorized the recitation in English and rehearsed it endlessly the night before.

When his father paused, Alexander translated the passage with a clipped, emphatic rhythm. "Declared on the Klingon Farm World Soch! A planet awarded to the Empire under the terms of the Organian Treaty of 2267. Where enemies with wounds still raw from war united to repel the invading Narr."

Catching his breath while Worf continued in Klingon, Alexander launched into the next passage feeling empowered by the passionate words.

"To honor Captain James T. Kirk, who fought for a world he was *not* sworn to defend."

Worf's powerful Klingon words echoed off the rafters.

"To honor Commander Kor," Alexander repeated the phrase in English. "Who recognized honor in an enemy and had the courage to risk his own for victory!"

"Batlh hoch yIn vI'tak je pol qaHegh 'Ip!"

Alexander's eyes narrowed and his own voice became harsh with menace as he delivered the final passage. "To honor *all* who live by truth and uphold to the *death* their given word!"

With the exception of Mr. Cunningham's jingling standard, absolute silence greeted the closing remark. Alexander suspected everyone was either too shocked by the reference to death or too intimidated by his father to risk offending him with applause. Or maybe they were just stunned to learn that the Federation's most notorious and honored starship captain, James T. Kirk, was responsible for the Klingon Empire's most respected holiday, too. Whatever the reason, their reaction would work to his advantage in the end.

The spotlights followed as Worf and Alexander moved to retrieve their *bat'leths*. The lights over the audience remained dark, but brightened over the stage area as father and son gripped the curved weapons with both hands and raised them above their heads.

"The *Suv'batlh* is fought when a warrior's honor is challenged by another." Worf's gaze scanned the darkened faces before him.

Alexander saw his opponents out of the corner of his eye. Sitting in chairs and visible in the dim light coming from the stage, Jeremy, Bernard and Kim stared at him with expressions ranging from cautious curiosity to wide-eyed terror to open hostility. Alexander smothered a smile and braced himself as his father went on.

"The ancient Honor Combat tests the courage of a warrior's heart as well as his skill!"

The metal standard sang as the science teacher shook the pole.

Taking the cue and moving in unison with his father, Alexander lowered his sword. He kept his eye on Worf's face as they both began to circle each other, swinging and dipping the deadly, pointed ends of the curved *bat'leths* in front of them. A rush of thrilled and anxious sound escaped the audience as Alexander suddenly spun, drew back and swung his blade overhand. Worf instantly raised his own blade to block the downward strike.

Alexander froze, holding his position.

Worf turned only his head to address the audience. "A Klingon warrior never resorts to deception when fighting the *Suv'batlh*. To evade by any devious means or trick would be dishonorable."

Instantly, Alexander pulled back and parried his father's series of side-to-side strikes. Metal clashed against metal until he stopped Worf's sword with a vertical block and froze once again.

"The *Suv'batlh* is *never* conceded." Worf snarled, causing the crowd to inhale with alarm. "It is *always* fought to the finish."

As lightning strikes—in a flash and without warning—Alexander leaped into action for the final, climactic sequence. Pushing his father's blade away, he circled and flipped the meter-long sword, then blocked Worf's overhand strike. Spinning around, he came out of the turn whipping his blade to the side. Worf blocked.

Alexander swung to the other side. Worf blocked, then drew back to land a resounding overhand strike against Alexander's defending blade. Then, as planned, Alexander lunged slightly, throwing his father "off balance." With a last, overhand swing of the *bat'leth,* he struck the "killing" blow to Worf's chest. As Worf fell, Mr. Santiago doused the lights.

Silence reigned as Worf got to his feet and raised his sword over his head to match Alexander's victorious stance. The hushed quiet erupted into cheers, whistles and thunderous applause when the lights came on again, revealing father and son in all their majestic Klingon glory.

Alexander noted that Mr. Houseman and his grandparents were applauding and grinning along with everyone else. His opponents' parents sat quietly, their expressions rigid and cold. Jeremy, Bernard and Kim seemed to be the only other spectators who hadn't thoroughly enjoyed the demonstration.

The hush that followed when the applause died down was one of tense anticipation rather than anxiety.

Cradling his sword in the curve of his arm, Alexander moved forward, then stood at attention as Worf placed his *bat'leth* back on the rack. He kept his eyes trained straight ahead when his father addressed the audience again.

"On his word of honor, Alexander Rozhenko has denied destroying the library bookcase."

Teachers and students frowned and a whisper of disturbed discussion swept the room.

"He refuses to name the persons who *are* guilty. Why?" Worf demanded, whirling to confront his son.

Alexander flinched even though he had expected the

question, but quickly recovered. "A heart without honor is hollow. To live without honor is to forsake self. To die without honor is to be forever reviled." He paused to let those words sink in before he concluded. "It would not be honorable to deny anyone their right to do the honorable thing and confess."

Alexander saw all three boys frown. Jeremy's expression was still hostile, Bernard's one of fear. Kim looked thoughtfully troubled.

Worf went on. "Alexander Rozhenko has been openly accused of starting a fight on school grounds. This he has also denied on his word of honor. Therefore, because his honor has been insulted, he has issued a challenge and the challenge has been accepted." Scowling ominously, Worf turned and pointed at the three boys. *"You* will come forward now and face the challenger!"

Behind him, Alexander heard the intense jangling of Mr. Cunningham's metal standard.

Murmurs of nervous surprise and fright rippled through the audience as Jeremy, Bernard and Kim stood up and slowly approached. Alexander did not meet their eyes as they paused before him, but he could tell that they were all scared. Even Jeremy's protective crust of smug confidence had crumbled.

"Honor will be restored to the victor and any request he makes will be granted." Worf looked at Alexander, then barked as he backed off. "Challenger! Choose your weapons and let the *Suv'batlh* begin!"

Alexander's eyes flashed as he instantly shifted his gaze to his opponents. Pressing the *bat'leth* over his head, he shouted and shook the sword. *"Batlh Daqawlu'jlH!"*

Bernard trembled. Jeremy tensed and Kim set his jaw.

All three boys turned white as the blood drained from their faces.

"Qab jlH nagil!" Alexander snarled. "I will be remembered with honor! Face me if you dare!" With a flourish, he whipped the sword up above his shoulder, intending to stay the blade.

The rage blindsided him as it burst free.

CHAPTER II

Alexander's arms trembled and his hands flexed on cold metal as he fought the savage command urging him to swing.

Jeremy and Kim cringed. Bernard ducked, throwing his arms over his head.

Gasps and cries of alarm rose from the assembly. Students jumped up in horrified disbelief and teachers glanced at each other uncertainly. Mr. Houseman, the office personnel and parents perched on the edge of their seats.

Filled with the power surging through his veins, Alexander felt the overwhelming desire of the Klingon predator to draw blood. He rebelled, calling on a stronger passion and a different strength. This was not a hunt and he was not a mindless beast. Clenching his teeth, he swung the sword and deftly pulled the swing, bringing the *bat'leth* to an abrupt halt in front of his chest. He stood perfectly still as he withdrew into himself and used the *Mok'bara* to calm the rage. Exhaling slowly, he turned, flipped the cutting edge toward him and offered the sword to Worf.

"The *Suv'batlh*," Alexander said, turning back to face the boys, "must be fought fairly if honor is to be served. These are the weapons I chose." As he pointed toward the far side of the gym, spotlights sudddenly illuminated the pommel horse, the high-bar and the vault.

The boys blinked in dazed confusion.

Jeremy recovered first and asked warily. "You're challenging us to a gymnastics meet?"

Alexander shrugged. "Well, if you'd rather settle this with *bat'leths*—"

His dark face shining with relief, Bernard emphatically shook his head. "Not me!"

Jeremy held up his hands. "I wouldn't mind learning how to use one, but right now—I'll pass."

Kim just smiled.

The crowd, suddenly realizing what had just happened, roared with approval as Alexander removed his wrist gauntlets and slipped out of the plated-metal chest armor. Then, motioning for the other three boys to go first, he followed them onto the gym floor where Ms. Petrovna directed them to halt and face the principal.

"In the interest of fairness," Mr. Houseman began, "we have invited three gymnastics coaches from other schools to judge the *Suv'batlh*."

Enthusiastic applause met the woman and two men who entered through a side door and seated themselves at a table. Their presence left no doubt that Alexander's choice of "weapons" had been planned and came as no surprise to the adults in charge.

Alexander glanced back at his father, who was watching intently with the *bat'leth* comfortably settled in his arm. He nodded slightly with a not-quite smile that warmed Alexander to the core. For Worf, it was the same as an ear-to-ear grin.

Smiling as she walked over to stand by Worf, Ms. Marconi gave him a thumbs-up. Mr. Cunningham winked and gently shook the bangled staff.

"Alexander will compete against a different one of his opponents in each event. Their scores will not be revealed until the match is finished. The highest total score wins." Mr. Houseman looked at the three other boys. "You may decide among yourselves who will compete in each event. However, you will all go first."

The boys conferred as Ms. Petrovna marched to the vault. When she blew her whistle, Bernard removed his shoes and socks and darted to the starting line.

In keeping with the spirit of human sports events, the crowd applauded and screamed encouragement.

Kicking off his own boots and socks, Alexander shook his arms and legs to limber up. The vault was the easiest of the three events. Although Bernard was athletic and fast, gymnastics was not his sport. Jeremy and Kim, however, were on the school gymnastics team. They were used to performing under pressure and both competed on the high-bar and pommel horse, the most difficult apparatus.

Silence fell as Bernard paused to take several deep breaths. Then he was off and running. He jumped, hit the leather vault with both hands and executed a single somersault. Taking a step to keep from falling on landing, he threw his arms in the air.

The spectators whistled and cheered even though Bernard had not attempted a difficult vault or performed perfectly. His father applauded wildly and his mom jumped up and down with excitement. With a broad grin, Bernard bowed and shook his fist in the air. He had met the Klingon challenge and survived.

Alexander returned Bernard's nod as they passed each other on his way to the vault. It was a small gesture, but it signified a measure of acceptance. Perhaps, Alexander thought as he paused on the line, his war against prejudice had already been won. If so, there would be no losers in the *Suv'batlh* being waged on the gym floor.

Focusing on the leather vault, Alexander drew a deep breath and took off at a run. With a flying leap, he hit the vault with his hands and pushed off into a perfect layout body turn and a solid landing. Straightening, Alexander punched the sky with his fists.

A silence even more absolute than the one after the Day of Honor origin recitation fell over the crowd. He held his pose, knowing his vault had been spectacular and his landing perfect. Still, maybe he had been right all along. Demonstrating his superior agility and strength would not ingratiate him to his human peers.

Then someone whooped and whistled from the bleachers. Within a split second, the gym filled with the thunder of clapping hands, shouts and whistles of enthusiastic appreciation. Worf roared with unabashed Klingon pride.

A shudder of emotion swept through Alexander and tears of joyous relief swelled in his eyes. Clamping down on the decidedly non-Klingon reaction and blinking back the mist, he smiled as he bowed and jogged back toward the others.

"That was perfect!" Bernard laughed.

"Very close anyway," Jeremy agreed, shaking his head in wonder. "Looks like we've got some *real* competition."

Kim nodded, then looked up as Ms. Petrovna moved to the high-bar and blew her whistle. With a curt salute that Alexander was sure included him, the slim boy ran to the mat.

"Go, Kim!" Alexander shouted.

Grinning, Jeremy and Bernard hooted encouragement.

Everyone lapsed into respectful silence again as Kim leaped to grab the bar. Swinging forward, then back to pick up momentum, he completed two rotations of the bar in exquisite form, then executed a handstand. On his downward swing, he released his hold, turned his body in the air and caught the bar again. As he swung over the top, he dismounted with a single somersault and nailed the landing.

As Alexander approached the bar, he couldn't help but be impressed with Kim's flawless routine. Scoring higher wouldn't be easy.

"The bar feels a little slippery," Kim said as he stepped off the mat. "Be careful."

"I will," Alexander said, his voice choked with shock. It was the first time Kim had ever spoken to him as a person and not an enemy. "Thanks."

"Sure." Smiling, Kim jogged away.

Dipping into the chalk bucket, Alexander dusted the excess carbonate of magnesium off his hands, then paused to breathe in deeply. He jumped, caught the bar and swung instantly into three rotations topped off with a handstand. As his body fell forward, he bent his legs into a pike position and slipped them through his arms, released and turned to catch the bar again. His left hand slipped. He managed to hang on, but the fluidity of his movement had been interrupted, which would cost him with the judges. Swinging his body up again, he released into a single somersault dismount and landed squarely on the mat.

No one seemed to care about Alexander's small mistake. Whether releasing their tension after the intensity of the Klingon segment of the program or just thoroughly enjoying a thrilling gymnastics competition, the crowd went wild.

"Too bad about that slip," Jeremy said when Alexander joined the group. "But I gotta warn you, the horse is my best event. I'm gonna try like crazy to beat you."

"Great. It wouldn't be any fun otherwise."

"Exactly." Responding to Ms. Petrovna's whistle, Jeremy dashed to the pommel horse in the center of the floor.

Jeremy paused to compose himself, then jumped and grabbed both pommels. With quick, sure releases of his hands as he moved, he swung his extended body to the left, then back to the center, then to the right, traveling the length of the horse. With both hands on the pommels again, he drew up into a handstand. Then, spreading his legs, he slowly lowered them until they extended in front of his body on either side of his arms. Swinging smoothly back into a handstand, he pushed off and nailed the landing. After saluting the audience with raised hands, Jeremy bowed then jumped with delight.

Alexander sighed, then headed across the gym. Jeremy had executed the difficult routine without a single glitch. There was only one way to beat him—if he dared.

"I think that's the best I've ever done, Alexander." Standing with his hands on his hips, Jeremy gasped for breath. "If you beat it, I'll—"

What? Alexander stiffened automatically.

"—buy your ticket to a holoflick in town tomorrow.

That new Ferengi comedy just started and Bernard and Kim are bustin' to see it."

"You're on!" Alexander beamed. Jeremy's proposal wasn't a dare or a gamble. It was just the boy's way of apologizing and opening the door to friendship. "And if I don't beat it, I'll buy for all three of you."

"Good luck." Cuffing Alexander's arm, Jeremy waved to a cheering audience as he left.

Recognizing an edge of nervousness that might distract him, Alexander paused and closed his eyes before starting. Using the *Mok'bara* discipline, he cleared his mind of everything except the pommel horse beside him. For a brief few moments, nothing else existed in his universe.

Grabbing the pommels, Alexander extended his legs and traveled the horse, demonstrating the same basic movements Jeremy had. Still following Jeremy's routine, he drew into a handstand, then scissored his legs. He followed through by slowly lowering his legs and holding position with them in front of his body. However, instead of finishing, he suddenly flashed into a difficult and complex movement known as the Thomas Flare since it had first been executed in a late twentieth-century Olympic Games. Whipping his scissored legs from one side to the other, he released and grabbed the pommels with lightning quickness. Then, with a burst of energy, he pushed off and dismounted with a half twist.

Alexander didn't need to hear the tumultuous roar of the crowd or see his father shaking the *bat'leth* in the air to know that his routine had been dazzling. If he had had any doubts, they would have been instantly vanquished as Jeremy, Bernard and Kim rushed up to surround him.

"I've never seen anyone do that before!" Bernard was breathless with excitement.

"Not in real life." Kim qualified the other boy's observation. "Only in *major* competitions."

"I'm so flabbergasted, I don't know what to say." Jeremy shrugged, then extended his hand.

Alexander shook it, making sure not to squeeze with the full power of his Klingon grip. Breaking Jeremy's hand at this point might end a wonderful friendship before it ever got started.

"Attention!" Mr. Houseman shouted, moving his arms in a downward motion as he tried to quiet the audience. "Please! May I have your attention!"

Ms. Petrovna blew her whistle and Mr. Santiago flashed the lights. Order returned within a minute.

"The results, if you will." Mr. Houseman glanced at the judges. The woman keyed a panel on the table. Each boy's total score flashed on the board attached high on the end wall.

Alexander's point total was higher by a wide margin.

With the *bat'leth* ceremoniously cradled in his arm, Worf, followed by Ms. Marconi with her light tech-torch and Mr. Cunningham with his jangling standard, came forward.

"The *Suv'batlh* has been fought and won!" Worf announced. "Alexander Rozhenko's honor has been avenged and restored."

Cheers and applause rose and quickly died when Worf frowned.

Alexander struggled to keep a straight face.

"Any request you make will be granted! *Yay'lIj!* Victory is yours!"

Alexander started uncertainly as all eyes focused on him. He hadn't really thought about the request part of the *Suv'batlh*. He already had everything he wanted—his honor and the respect of his father and peers. Still, one thing suddenly came to mind.

"I would like to try out for the gymnastics team."

Mr. Santiago jumped to his feet. "You've got it, Alexander! See me right after school."

"Uh . . ." Alexander's cheeks flushed slightly. "I can't. I've got detention."

Silence.

"No!" Glancing at Kim and Bernard, Jeremy stepped forward. "We tipped over that bookcase, not Alexander."

"And we started the fight!" Kim added.

"We're the ones who should be punished," Bernard concluded.

Alexander stared. The *Batlh Jaj* ceremony had apparently been far more impressive than he had imagined.

Mr. Houseman rubbed his chin, then looked up with a smile. "In keeping with Klingon tradition, the *Suv'batlh* has settled these matters. We'll just call it even. As long as—" He scowled pointedly at all three boys. "—you promise not to do anything like this again."

"Word of honor!" The boys swore in unison, raising their right hands as was the human custom.

"Dismissed." Mr. Houseman grinned.

And Mr. Cunningham jangled the standard one last time.

As the students and teachers began to file out to return to class, the boys' parents and the Rozhenkos hurried over to congratulate the contestants.

"You were magnificent, Alexander!" Sergey beamed.

Mr. Sullivan clasped Jeremy by the arms. "I'm proud of you, son. You may have the makings of a good Starfleet officer after all."

"Thanks, Dad."

"Alexander is thinking about going to Starfleet Academy, too." Helena smiled, her eyes twinkling.

Alexander gasped. He had never, ever told anyone he wanted to join Starfleet. The idea had never entered his mind. "Who told you that?"

"Your father!" Helena said brightly. "He told me that you said you wanted to be just like him. He's so proud."

"But did he say Starfleet specifically?" Alexander pressed. It hadn't been that long since Worf had stopped trying to push him into a Klingon way of life. He didn't think he could stand it if his father suddenly started pushing him toward Starfleet.

Helena frowned. "Specifically? No, I don't believe he did."

Alexander sagged in relief. For a long time he had thought he wanted to be a diplomat like his mother, K'Ehleyr. They shared the mixed human and Klingon heritage that had allowed her to be so effective in trying to bridge the gap between the Federation and the Empire. Recently, though, he had come to realize that his interest in that career path had been greatly influenced by his father's stubborn determination to turn him into a Klingon warrior. In truth, he knew that K'Ehleyr wouldn't want him to become a diplomat for her sake any more than she had wanted him to become a warrior to please Worf. To make his mother truly proud, he would have to find his own path—whatever it was. He had plenty of time to decide whether he wanted to be a diplomat or a Klingon warrior or a Starfleet officer or something else entirely. Right now, he just wanted to be a kid.

A mostly Klingon kid living in a human world, he realized soberly. He would never be free of the savage rage that lurked in his Klingon blood. For the rest of his life he would have to guard and struggle against his natural tendency to fight first and think later. However, now he knew he *could* conquer those powerful, warrior impulses just as his father had.

Feeling better about himself than he had in a long time, Alexander looked at the students leaving the gym. He inhaled softly when he caught Suzanne Milton staring at him.

Alexander snarled, then smiled.

Suzanne flushed, waved shyly and smiled back.

Glancing over his shoulder, Alexander watched as his father demonstrated how to use a *bat'leth* for Ms. Marconi. However, the librarian's rapt attention was on Worf and not the sword.

Starfleet officer and Klingon warrior.

Alexander frowned thoughtfully. He had to admit there were advantages to being both.

About the Author

Diana G. Gallagher lives in Minnesota with her husband, Marty Burke, three dogs, three cats, and a cranky parrot. When she's not writing, she likes to read, walk the dogs, and look for cool stuff at garage sales for her grandsons, Jonathan, Alan, and Joseph.

Diana and Marty are musicians who perform traditional and original Irish and American folk music at coffeehouses and conventions around the country. Marty sings and plays the twelve-string guitar and banjo. In addition to singing backup harmonies, Diana plays rhythm guitar and a round Celtic drum called a *bodhran*.

A Hugo Award–winning artist, Diana is best known for her series *Woof: The House Dragon.* Her first adult novel, *The Alien Dark,* appeared in 1990. She and Marty coauthored *The Chance Factor,* a STARFLEET ACADEMY VOYAGER book. In addition to other STAR TREK novels for intermediate readers, Diana has written many books in other series published by Minstrel Books, including *The Secret World of Alex Mack, Are You Afraid of the Dark,* and *The Mystery Files of Shelby Woo.* She is currently working on original young adult novels for the Archway Paperback series, *Sabrina, the Teenage Witch.*

About the Illustrator

Gordon Purcell received B.A.'s in studio arts and theatre from the University of Minnesota and has been a working commercial artist ever since. He is best known for his comic book artwork, including the following titles: DEEP SPACE NINE (Malibu Comics). STAR TREK, STAR TREK: THE NEXT GENERATION and FLASH (DC Comics), SILVER SABLE, MAD DOG and THE AVENGERS (Marvel), and BARB WIRE and YOUNG INDIANA JONES (Dark Horse). He currently draws THE X-FILES comic for Topps. He lives it up outside Minneapolis with lovely wife, Debra, and wonder-child, Jack.

**Beam aboard for a special trilogy
featuring Cadet Kathryn Janeway!**

STAR TREK®
VOYAGER™
STARFLEET ACADEMY®

**Read about Captain Janeway's
Starfleet Academy adventures!**

#1 *LIFELINE*
By Bobbi JG Weiss and David Cody Weiss

#2 *THE CHANCE FACTOR*
By Diana G. Gallagher and Martin R. Burke

#3 *QUARANTINE*
By Patricia Barnes-Svarney

A MINSTREL® BOOK

Published by Pocket Books   1378

#1 THE TALE OF THE SINISTER STATUES 52545-X/$3.99
#2 THE TALE OF CUTTER'S TREASURE 52729-0/$3.99
#3 THE TALE OF THE RESTLESS HOUSE 52547-6/$3.99
#4 THE TALE OF THE NIGHTLY NEIGHBORS 53445-9/$3.99
#5 THE TALE OF THE SECRET MIRROR 53671-0/$3.99
#6 THE TALE OF THE PHANTOM SCHOOL BUS 53672-9/$3.99
#7 THE TALE OF THE GHOST RIDERS 56252-5/$3.99
#8 THE TALE OF THE DEADLY DIARY 53673-7/$3.99
#9 THE TALE OF THE VIRTUAL NIGHTMARE 00080-2/$3.99
#10 THE TALE OF THE CURIOUS CAT 00081-0/$3.99
#11 THE TALE OF THE ZERO HERO 00357-7/$3.99
#12 THE TALE OF THE SHIMMERING SHELL 00392-5/$3.99
#13 THE TALE OF THE THREE WISHES 00358-5/$3.99
#14 THE TALE OF THE CAMPFIRE VAMPIRES 00908-7/$3.99
#15 THE TALE OF THE BAD-TEMPERED GHOST 01429-3/$3.99

A MINSTREL BOOK